"DONNA . . ." HE BEGAN AS HE CAME CLOSER TO HER.

"Don't come near me!" she snapped furiously. "You—oh, I don't even know what to call you! You knew all the while that I came from an extremely religious home, and you led me to believe you were a Catholic priest! How could you? And you had the nerve to find it all amusing—"

"Donna!" he interrupted her, and she knew that her rising temper had set a flame to his. "I just let you go by your own self-righteous assumptions."

"Self-righteous assumptions!" she exclaimed. "My assumptions weren't self-righteous. They were natural. And you know it! You knew exactly what I thought and how I would ~~feel~~. And then last night—oh, I know precisely what ~~~~ you are a selfish~~~~ ow-blooded heel!"

D1115590

CANDLELIGHT ECSTASY ROMANCES®

SENSUOUS ANGEL

Heather Graham

A CANDLELIGHT ECSTASY ROMANCE®

Published by
Dell Publishing Co., Inc.
1 Dag Hammarskjold Plaza
New York, New York 10017

For Al and Lena, "Nana" and "Papa" Pozzessere, with lots of love

Copyright © 1985 by Heather E. Graham

All rights reserved. No part of this book may be reproduced
or transmitted in any form or by any means, electronic
or mechanical, including photocopying, recording, or by any
information storage and retrieval system, without the written
permission of the Publisher, except where permitted by law.

Dell ® TM 681510, Dell Publishing Co., Inc.

Candlelight Ecstasy Romance®, 1,203,540, is a registered
trademark of Dell Publishing Co., Inc., New York, New York.

ISBN: 0-440-17636-0

Printed in the United States of America

First printing—August 1985

To Our Readers:

We have been delighted with your enthusiastic response to Candlelight Ecstasy Romances®, and we thank you for the interest you have shown in this exciting series.

In the upcoming months we will continue to present the distinctive sensuous love stories you have come to expect only from Ecstasy. We look forward to bringing you many more books from your favorite authors and also the very finest work from new authors of contemporary romantic fiction.

As always, we are striving to present the unique, absorbing love stories that you enjoy most—books that are more than ordinary romance.

Your suggestions and comments are always welcome. Please write to us at the address below.

Sincerely,

The Editors
Candlelight Romances
1 Dag Hammarskjold Plaza
New York, New York 10017

PROLOGUE

May 5
Dear Donna,

New York, New York! "It's my kind of town"! Or is that supposed to be Chicago? I can't remember, but I am in New York and awfully glad to be here. Different scenery, etc., etc. I'm not sure what I want to do yet, but I guess I've got time. I'm going to be a tourist for the next few weeks. Having never been here before, I'm absolutely fascinated. Today the Empire State building, tomorrow the world.

Anyway, I am well and doing fine. How about yourself? Anything new? Write soon. Luv ya,

Lorna

June 1
Dear Lorna,

You sound great! And I'm sorry, but "My kind of town" is Chicago. But that's all right. New York is a "wonderful lady" and I'm sure it will be wonderful for you. It's so hectic there that you really can forget anything painful and go on. Keep in touch; call if you get the urge. If I can, I'll come down to meet you soon.

Donna

June 20
Dear Donna,

Radio City Music Hall and a half dozen museums later, I'm still in love with New York. Of course, I've been all over by now! I've seen the grand—and an awful lot of the very seedy. But I'm still doing fine. And I'm eager to see you when you get here. Hurry up and get some of that olive oil out of your hands so that you can come down and meet me. I'll teach you how to ice skate a whole new way at Rockefeller Plaza.

Lorna

July 10
Dear Lorna,

Well, it hasn't really been the "olive oil" keeping me, and you know it. But guess what? I'm an official "Miss" once again. It seems crazy to have been "married" less than a month—and then have it take over two years to finish with the paperwork. A divorce would have taken about eight weeks, they say, but I guess I'm glad I filed for the annulment. It meant so much to the family, and I didn't want to do anything else right away. Not after Mark. This "olive oil" you're teasing me about helped keep me sane!

But anyway, I found out the other day that the annulment went through Rome last February. I will be very officially single when I meet you—soon. I promise.

Donna

July 28
Donna!

Oh, my God! Can things happen here! Just a quick note to say I'm glad that things worked out—but don't come here! I met the strangest man, and suddenly things went berserk. If I wanted danger and excitement, I guess I've got it now. But that's New York—you never know what might happen when you walk down the street. I sound like I'm babbling, don't I? But I'm frightened silly. I have to put my trust in Andrew McKennon—even though he can be a true SOB! I want to strangle the man half the time, but then again . . . well, he is trying to help me now. I haven't any other choice. I know this sounds crazy, but right now I can't explain the rest because I don't know what is going on myself. Donna—sit tight. I'll write again when I can. One day I'll be able to tell you all about this and maybe then I'll be able to laugh. No, I won't ever be able to laugh. Oh, what a mess! Think of me, pray for me! But please don't worry.

Lorna

August 5
Lorna! Lorna!

"Please don't worry"! You've made me crazy!

What are you trying to do to me? You have me scared witless! What are you talking about and what is going on? Call me—as soon as you get this. Don't you dare write to me again on hospital stationery and not say anything. Please, please, call me, Lorna, so that I know you are all right. I'm not even sure that my letters reach you—you keep changing addresses every time you write. Lorna, I'm begging you, give me a call. Alexander Graham Bell invented the telephone for occasions just like this! Please, Lorna!

Donna

August 12
Dear Miss Miro:

I'm very sorry, but Lorna can't call or write to you now. Please be patient. She'll get in touch with you as soon as she can. You are trying to involve yourself in something that you don't understand; please, for your own safety and Lorna's, just be patient and wait. You will hear from her soon.

Andrew McKennon

August 14
AIR EXPRESS
MR. McKENNON:

I want to hear from Lorna *right now.* Today. I want to

know what is going on. If not, I'll have private detectives on the case immediately.

Donna Miro

AUGUST 15
RETURN TO SENDER
UNDELIVERABLE AS ADDRESSED
NO SUCH PERSON AT THIS ADDRESS

CHAPTER ONE

Mile after mile of tenements seemed to reach into space endlessly, sliding into infinity as the stars in the heavens.

But this was no heavenly abode. Nor could it stretch forever, no matter how it seemed. Not far away, Donna knew, the lights of Broadway glittered down on the "beautiful" people, the diamonds of the rich, the sables, foxes, and minks coming into use as fall lowered its gentle hand over the steaming summer heat of the concrete jungle known as Manhattan. Land of ten million people, the Stock Exchange, the theater, the United Nations. The hub of hustling, teeming, ever-moving business. Central Park, Saks Fifth Avenue. And countless ghettos.

The crumbling facades of the neck-to-neck buildings Donna studiously scanned were withered and brown, swallowing what remained of the twilight, appearing to wait like mammoth monsters to pounce on the unwary. They reeked of dismal nightlife, of things done beneath the cover of darkness. It was almost as if the tenements silently laughed, waiting to open their arms and welcome all strays into a den of cutthroats, harlots, and thieves.

"And your imagination is incredible!" Donna whispered aloud to herself with annoyance. The tenements were nothing but housing for the poor, pathetic housing where the rats and graffiti battled for space.

Still, as she walked, she wished fervently that she had taken care of her business during the day. She had been so sure that she could read a map, that she knew what she was doing, that a cab would whiz by at any time she decided she needed one. But it was apparent that cab drivers didn't cater to this neighborhood and just as apparent that she didn't know what she was doing. She had read the map. But although it pointed out Saint

13

Patrick's Cathedral, the Metropolitan Museum, and even Macy's, it did not point to this row upon row of tenements and warn: Detour! Dangerous ghetto!

Whom had she been fooling? she wondered now with growing dismay. A private detective had failed to find Lorna; even the police were behaving as if Lorna had never existed. They had told Donna quite flatly that no such person as Andrew McKennon had ever lived in New York.

It was growing darker and darker. Although her heels clicked bravely against the pavement, Donna was beginning to know fear. Belatedly she was remembering crime statistics, and that she was there in the first place because the city was famous for beckoning the unwary . . . sucking them up like quicksand.

There goes my imagination again! she silently chastised herself. No, it wasn't really imagination. Lorna had come to the city and it might as well have swallowed her whole. There was no trace of Lorna Doria.

Something strange had happened to Lorna, yes. But Lorna had *not* walked down the street and been swallowed whole by a row of tenements. The tenements only *seemed* to be alive, breathing with evil menace, because Donna was, admittedly, frightened—and allowing her imagination to run riot. Lorna's disappearance was a mystery—but logic clearly informed Donna that the street, which wasn't alive or evil, had done nothing to Lorna. It was just a street. A sad street. And surely no one would bother Donna either.

Or would they? Was she crazy? Or did she really hear the light fall of footsteps behind her? Donna paused, ostensibly adjusting the shoe strap around her heel. She barely breathed as she tried to listen. There was nothing, nothing but the distant sounds of the city, muted taxi horns, fading rock music. She started walking again.

She hadn't realized her quest would bring her directly into the ghetto, but she had instinctively dressed for anonymity. She wore a severe navy-blue business suit with a plain white tailored blouse. Her hair was tied in a chignon at her nape, its sable length austerely hidden. Her features were fine-boned, clearly cut—almost fragile—but she had learned long ago to face the world with sharp blue eyes and challenge. Despite the delicacy

14

of her five-foot-four frame, few would ever think her lacking the will of a polite, civilized tigress.

Except that right now, Donna Miro wasn't feeling much like a tigress. She was wishing that rather than being the possessor of a truckload of business acumen, she had elected to take Karate 101 back at the university. At first she had only suspected she was being followed; she had rationalized the feeling by convincing herself it was a natural, if unfounded, fear.

Now she stopped again, this time adjusting the heel strap on her other shoe, and now there was no rationalization for her fear. It wasn't unfounded. Above the distant, muted din of the city, she heard something else. Much nearer. Too near. She was sure she was being followed.

Stealthy footsteps could be heard behind her. And ahead of her all that loomed was shadow, as if the hulking tenements lurked, waiting with their embrace of darkness . . . of evil. . . .

Donna quickened her pace as pinpricks of fear assailed her, ripping along the length of her spine with the same subtle whisper of the night sounds that breathed danger. Sounds that echoed and grew in her mind, sounds that mocked the self-assurance of her almost three decades of life.

Yes, she was definitely being followed. Glancing over her shoulder, Donna was just in time to see a shadow blend into a wall. She quickened her pace again until her clicking pace was almost a jog.

There were no more soft whispers of warning. The footsteps were no longer stealthy. Their pace quickened in time with hers, drowning out all else. They rang loud and clear in the cool stillness of the night. Their beat on the pavement spoke of one intent—to outdistance, to overpower. The shadow behind her was now oblivious to exposure.

Donna glanced back once more. The figure was coming after her full speed. She couldn't best that speed in heels, nor could she take the time to discard her shoes. She screamed, but as in a dream, the sound was weak. It was a croak. She hugged her shoulder bag to her and ran, adrenaline providing a burst of energy.

But escape was impossible. Her assailant was upon her, catching her arm, spinning her about in a crazy circle that

15

caught her heel and cruelly twisted her ankle. She was staring at him with wide eyes. Despite her panic, she realized that the man was really a youth, but a street-wise youth, fleet on his feet, sure of his trade. He could disappear back into the shadows just as easily as he had come when he was done with her.

Done what with her? she wondered desperately. She panicked and began to struggle fiercely, raining blows against his leather jacket. How ridiculous, she thought vaguely in a vain attempt to still her terror. She should be able to stop him. He had to be almost ten years younger than she.

"Hey, mama, just the bag, baby, just the bag," the kid hissed.

Donna struggled then to loosen her arm from the shoulder bag, gasping as she saw the gleaming blade of a knife in the last glitters of twilight.

"Please!" Donna gasped in sudden horror. What the hell was she doing? Fighting over her purse! Give him the damn thing, she warned herself. It had just been natural instinct to fight, but now she tried to force herself to reason. To remember. In such a situation, she shouldn't fight. She should just hand the bag over and start praying that she got out of the situation unharmed.

He was carrying a knife—a knife!

"I'll give it to you," she stated, aware that her voice faltered as she fumbled to hand him the bag.

She was even more terrified than she had realized. She dropped the bag. He seemed to emit an animal growl, and she dodged to retrieve it as the knife flashed beneath her eyes. "No tricks, baby, no tricks."

She picked up the bag and handed it to him. He laughed, catching her arm again and pulling her close. He gave her an evil grin, which displayed yellowing teeth. "Oh, little mama! Jungle George don't wanta hurt you, baby. Not unless you like it that way. Naw . . . baby . . . ol' George can think of lots better things to do."

She was going to pass out, Donna thought with horror as the twilight swam to darkness before her. "Let me go . . ." she echoed weakly. She went rigid, telling herself he was a teenager. She shouldn't sound like a simpering fool; she should use a voice of authority. Because they weren't talking about her purse anymore. They were talking about life and death, physical harm, rape. . . .

16

"Let go of me!" she snapped more strongly. "You've got my purse; take it and run. Leave me alone. Are you aware of the repercussions, the legal repercussions—"

"Are you aware, mama, that this blade could slide across your throat in a second?"

"Let me go," Donna repeated quietly, firmly, giving no indication of the rampant shivers within her.

"Go . . . yeah, let's go for a little walk—"

Her assailant's words were cut off suddenly, as if his sentence had been severed by a steel blade. Donna was released so abruptly that she staggered and—unable to find her balance on her twisted ankle—fell to the sidewalk. Gasping with shock, Donna blinked and inhaled deeply and realized that another shadow had appeared in the night. A towering shadow in black that now wrenched her assailant about with the force of a tornado. Stunned, Donna watched as the youth was yanked by the scruff of the neck and pinioned to a crumbling wall, his toes not quite touching the ground.

"Not in my neighborhood, macho man, do you hear?" the new figure demanded in a chilling baritone. "Not in my neighborhood."

"Let me go!" the kid hissed. "Hey, man, I got me a blade. I ain't never sliced me a pr—"

"Drop the knife, man," the towering, black-clad form mocked threateningly, "before you wind up wearing the damn thing all the way to hell."

The knife clattered to the pavement. As much as the threat, the man's language shocked the kid to silence. It also shocked Donna into a breathless immobility as she realized that the tall, broad-shouldered man pinioning the wiry youth to the wall with one hand and speaking in the low, deathly tones was a priest. Black shirt, black jacket, white collar. . . . Yes, he was a priest, who wore black with almost sinful appeal, that very black emphasizing the rugged contours of a strong, trim, and yet well muscled body—a very healthy physique. A black that blended with that of a handsome head of thick dark hair, that contrasted sharply with strange hazel eyes—a hazel that gleamed golden in the night, like all the fires of hell. . . .

Still sprawled on the ground, Donna was too transfixed to attempt to stand, too shocked to even assimilate her relief and

17

gratitude at the timely rescue. She could only stare at the strange pair before her as the incredible action unfolded.

"You can't hit me!" the teenager whined. "It's against your religion."

"Like bloody damned hell I can't," the priest warned with a wicked chuckle. "God is a real terror in the Old Testament, son. Vengeful guy. An eye for an eye and all that. He flooded the world and made rubble of Sodom and Gomorrah. I'm sure he'll be real understanding if I just break the neck of one little sneak thief."

"Please . . . I wasn't going to hurt nobody," the youth managed in a strangled gasp. "See, I just needed the bread. Times are hard, Father. . . ."

"Really?" the priest inquired, deceptively polite. "Strange—I heard you definitely threatening the lady."

"No . . . I was just scaring her a little. Really, Father. Hey, I ain't no rapist. And my record's clean. I swear it. I'll swear it on a thousand Bibles."

"Tell me about the 'little walk' you were about to take. A knife—that's armed robbery, macho man."

"No, Father, really." There were tears in the boy's eyes now. Donna felt an absurd twinge of pity; he was in deeper terror now than she had been when the knife had been at her throat. And he was young. Really young. Just a kid. . . .

"I just wanted to get closer to the shadows of the buildings, Father. So's I could let her go and then disappear with no chance of her getting a cop on me. I swear to God, Father! I swear. I'll never do it again, Father, never—"

"Get out of here!" the priest commanded with disgust, shoving the youth from him. "I won't call the cops—this time. But if I ever see you doing anything other than helping old ladies across the street again, I promise you'll be in agony when you do sit in your jail cell—got it?"

Dumbfounded still and probably scared into ten years of penitence, the boy nodded fervently. His face was as ashen as the crumbling facades of the tenements.

"Padre, I'll find a job. I promise. I ain't never gonna steal again, I swear it. May God strike me dead—"

"If you're serious, call the rectory. No promises, but maybe there might be something. Now, go!" the priest commanded.

Still the youth hesitated, the tears streaming down his cheeks. "Padre—"

"No one's coming after you, son," the priest said with a quiet sigh. "I'm going to trust your promises. Partly because I don't think you'd chance another run-in with me. Now—go on! Go home!"

The youth began to back away, slinking against the wall. He moved hesitantly at first, then—as soon as he had gained a safe distance from the priest—he turned and began to run as if all the demons of hell were after him.

The priest watched him until he was swallowed up by the shadows of twilight. His face as ruggedly immobile as granite, he stooped and retrieved the offending knife with an agility that was startling for his size. He tripped the blade and folded it into his pocket. Then his disturbing golden gaze turned to Donna.

He crossed his arms over his chest and stared down at her, annoyance clearly etched across his well-defined and rakishly handsome features.

"All right, lady," he demanded impatiently. "Just what kind of an idiot are you?"

She was no less stunned by the strange priest than her assailant.

CHAPTER TWO

"I'm not an idiot!" Donna protested indignantly. She winced inwardly. Sprawled on the ground, her stockings ripped, her neat chignon a mass of tangled dishevelment, she did feel a bit like a fool, if not a complete idiot. But she was not about to condescend the point to this man—even if he had rescued her and even if he was a priest.

He shook his head with exasperation. "Lady, any woman walking along this street in a suit from Saks has to be an idiot." He finally extended his hand to her. She gazed stupidly at his hand. It was broad, the fingers long, the nails bluntly clipped.

Ignoring his gesture, she attempted to rise on her own. As soon as she placed her weight on her injured ankle, a streak of pain ripped through her. Before she could stop it, a soft cry escaped her. To her vast dismay, she found she was losing her balance once more.

But before she could teeter ignominiously back to the pavement again, the supporting hand she had just refused came about her waist and she was steadied. She stared up into the flame hazel eyes that now held a glint of amusement and murmured an awkward "Thank you."

It was the most disconcerting gaze she had ever encountered —and from a priest. "I—I can stand now," she stuttered nervously.

He chuckled. "And then what?"

"Pardon?"

"It's unlikely that you can walk."

"I'll just get a cab—"

"Don't be a fool."

A flash of anger ripped through her. "I'm already an idiot. Why not be a fool?"

He chuckled again, undaunted by her wrath. "Why not indeed?" But before Donna could respond, she found herself lifted into strong arms and secured against his broad chest, and held with no more effort than he might expend on a feather as his long stride took them down the street.

"Wait . . ." Donna protested feebly. "I have to find a man—"

"You'll find lots of men if you keep this up."

"Damn it! I mean—"

He started to laugh. "Calm down—just for a few minutes. You're not going to do anything in the state you ARE in so listen to me and be agreeable. Didn't anyone ever tell you that the *meek* shall inherit'?"

"No—and they obviously forgot to tell you!"

He inclined his head slightly, his too-sensual lips curving subtly. Then he ignored her comment. "You can explain what the hell you think you're doing, and then maybe I can help you. You're definitely not going anywhere on your own power with that ankle," he said matter-of-factly.

Donna's arms had instinctively wound around his neck when he had lifted her. She sighed softly, biting back further reply. It wasn't the most normal feeling in the world to want to throttle a priest, and she had to admit that, thanks to him, she was in fairly good health and still in possession of her shoulder bag. And she hadn't even thanked him. Of course, he wasn't the type to draw out profuse gratitude. She relaxed suddenly, closing her eyes, aware—not without a certain resentment—that he was right. If he had left her, she would have truly been in trouble: lost in the ghetto and unable to walk.

And maybe—just maybe—this man could help her. He obviously knew the neighborhood. If she didn't accept his help now, she really would be an idiot. She was still shaking from her encounter with the youthful assailant. At this particular moment, it was pure relief to forget her quest, to lean on his masculine strength.

Her eyes flew open. His masculine strength! The man was a priest! Oh, dear Lord! she thought dismally. What were you thinking when you made this man a priest?

21

He was almost a foot taller than she, and built solidly. He wasn't heavy, but touching him she knew he was all muscle. His scent was light but pleasantly masculine, the hair her fingers brushed at his nape was decidedly, satanically dark. The jaw she stared up at was determinedly strong and square, and the eyes that occasionally glanced down to hers were the most wickedly compelling and . . . seductive . . . she had ever seen.

Donna lowered her eyes uncomfortably, flushing suddenly with acute and painful embarrassment. She didn't remember ever being so affected by a man—not even the one man she had, however briefly, called her husband. Even the touch of his jacket against her cheek seemed to send shivers racing along her spine. Guilt riddled her along with the shivers. She'd spent half her life in Catholic schools, and there she was reacting physically to a man of the cloth.

No! It was only an aftereffect, she told herself staunchly. And for a priest, he was terribly rude and abusive. He had called her an idiot, and she was not an idiot!

Still, she gritted her teeth as he turned one corner and then another. They hadn't come far at all, but suddenly they were out of the ghetto, facing Central Park.

"I—I'm sure I can get a cab here," she stuttered.

"I'll get a cab," he said curtly.

It seemed he had no sooner said the words than a taxi was pulling up beside them. She was placed inside it, and then he was sliding next to her. He gave the driver an address that meant nothing to her.

"Really," Donna began, feeling as if her nerves were pulled like a guitar string, "I'm sorry I've troubled you. I'll just go to my hotel room."

"No way, lady." The priest chuckled. "I don't want to spend all my days walking the streets. Let's solve your problem tonight so that I don't have to worry about picking you up in pieces some night."

Donna clamped her lips tightly together. "I am not an idiot," she said quietly. "I ran into a bit of bad luck, that's all."

He didn't respond. The cab came to a halt on a pretty, tree-lined street with ivy-covered brownstones.

"I'll pay for the cab," Donna said quickly, scrambling in her purse for the fare.

"I think I can handle it," the priest said dryly, handing the driver a number of bills.

The cabbie smiled in return. "Thanks, Father Luke."

"Have a good night, Jonas," he said briefly, and then he was reaching for Donna again, lifting her from the cab before she could protest.

"I really do think I could hobble along," Donna said awkwardly as he walked her up a flight of immaculately clean steps and pressed a buzzer. She flushed as his gaze fell on her. There was something about his subtle smile and the devilish gleam in his magnetic gold and green eyes that told her quite blatantly he was fully aware of her discomfort from his touch—and very amused by it.

The door suddenly swung inward and they were greeted with startled surprise by a squat little woman who barely reached the priest's broad shoulders. "Luke! My goodness! What has happened? Bring the poor girl in right away and I'll get some tea on. There's a fire in your office, Father. Oh, my, my! Should I call the doctor?"

"I don't think that will be necessary, Mary. I believe the lady merely has a slight sprain."

"I'll get a tub of hot water and epsom salts then, Father."

"Thank you, Mary."

"Oh, please!" Donna protested, feeling truly absurd as she nestled in the priest's strong arms and stared into the warm brown eyes of the kindly and concerned housekeeper. "Please don't put yourself to any trouble! I'm sure I'll be fine."

"No trouble at all, young lady," Mary said firmly. "Come along now, Luke—let's get that sprain taken care of!"

Father Luke followed his housekeeper meekly down a hall attractively furnished with a dark crimson rug and an antique deacon's bench to a door just past the bannistered stairway.

"Whatever happened?" Mary queried again as she pushed the door inward and stood aside so that the priest could set Donna in a large plush sofa.

"Our young friend stumbled upon one of our more dangerous streets," the priest offered wryly, leaving Donna as he stood casually against the corner of a massive oak desk.

23

"Oh, no! You were mugged! Poor dear!"

"I really am fine," Donna said meekly, wishing for some reason that she could dig a hole beneath the sofa rather than lie on it.

Mary was *tsk*ing away. "I'll get the tea and epsom salts right away, Miss—" She stopped, staring awkwardly at Father Luke.

He shrugged and lifted his hands casually. "I don't know her name, Mary. She hasn't offered to tell me."

Donna wondered briefly how great a sin it was to wish to boil a priest in bubbling oil. She forced a smile to her lips. "Miro," she told the housekeeper. "Donna Miro."

"Oh—you're Italian, aren't you?" Mary didn't wait for Donna's nod but rushed on. "I just knew it! You look just like Sophia Loren—when she was young, of course. Doesn't she, Luke?"

Luke now had his arms crossed over his chest as he freely surveyed Donna. His expression was grave; only his golden eyes gave away his humor. "Mmm—I suppose, Mary. But . . . not quite. The eyes are much more Elizabeth Taylor—when she was young, of course."

"You're so right, Luke!" Mary laughed. Then she smiled quickly at Donna and left the room, closing the door behind her.

Donna knew that she resembled a ripe tomato, her blush was so hot. She was both furious and incredibly at a loss. She was usually quite competent when dealing with men on business and socially, but this man was making her feel as if she were sixteen again.

And of all things, he was a priest. She had spent her life amidst a very Italian, very Catholic family. Priests were not supposed to be devastatingly handsome. Nor were they supposed to have shoulders like Sherman tanks nor possess eyes that touched one like fires.

"Well, Miss Miro? Or is it 'Mrs.'? Or 'Ms.'?"

Donna scrambled to sit up, forcing herself to meet the priest's eyes with a straightforward composure.

"Miro is my family name," she said curtly.

He cocked a brow politely and Donna fervently wished that she had simply chosen one of the above.

"You were never married?" he inquired.

24

It was none of his business! she thought resentfully. But there was something about that white collar—she couldn't lie or even evade.

"Once."

"But no more?"

"No more."

"Who were you looking for, Ms. Miro, and why?"

The change in the tenor of questioning came so abruptly that Donna found herself momentarily tongue-tied. Then she blurted out the name that was an anathema to her lips. "A man named Andrew McKennon."

The lids closed briefly over the priest's strange golden eyes; other than that, he gave no visible sign of any emotion.

"Do you know him?" Donna demanded. It seemed almost impossible; there were over eight million people in New York City—at least that was the conservative estimate—and it seemed that she had at last stumbled on a man who had heard of Andrew McKennon.

"Why are you looking for him?" the priest cross-queried.

Donna hesitated a moment. She wasn't accustomed to discussing her business with strangers, even if the stranger was a priest. And she was afraid she'd get the same answer she had gotten from the police—that she was probably worried over nothing. Lorna was an adult; it was her choice to disappear if she chose to.

The police had been sadly uninterested with the whole affair. But then it was hard to blame them. According to the harried officer who had assisted her, thousands of people were reported missing weekly.

"Ms. Miro?"

He was waiting for an answer. She was going to have to tell him something.

"A friend of mine disappeared here. The last letter I received from her mentioned a man named Andrew McKennon. Then I got a letter from McKennon himself, basically telling me to mind my own business."

The priest raised a dark brow and it seemed that a faint smile played about his lips. "But I take it that you don't think you can mind your own business?"

"Father, I'm concerned, very concerned. Lorna wrote to me

25

from a hospital—the hospital has no record of her ever being there. I wrote to the return address on the letter McKennon had sent me and my letter was returned. I hired a private detective to find Lorna—he could come up with nothing. Then I came myself. I haunted the police station. They were barely interested in letting me fill out the missing persons form. Lorna mentioned that she was in danger. If she told me that she was in danger, how can I forget about it? Maybe she's in over her head. Maybe she's involved with people that no one should be involved with! I have to find out who this McKennon is! He could be a criminal, a drug addict, a murderer for all I know!"

"Do you think that your friend would have involved herself with a man if he were a criminal?"

"Not purposely, no."

"But maybe she has gone away just because she wanted to."

"And maybe she hasn't. Father, if she had just decided to go away, she would have told me that. Damn it—she had already gone away from home! She was widowed about a year ago, and she came to New York for a change of pace. Father, she is worth quite a bit of money. I'm very afraid that she might be the victim of . . ."

"Of what?"

"Oh, I'm not sure! But some kind of foul play. And would you please stop with the questions! I asked you one."

"Ah, yes, you did."

"Well?"

"You asked me about Andrew McKennon?"

The words were softly voiced. Was he asking her, or telling her? Procrastinating?

"Yes, about McKennon!" she snapped, wishing fervently that she could shake the man. He did know something, she was certain. He was holding back. Playing with her in a strange fashion. Or else he was seeking information, just as she was.

"You do know him!" she exclaimed in accusation. "Why are you denying it?"

He half smiled, his features twisted into a handsome mask of subtle amusement. "I never denied it."

"Then please—tell me how to find him. Can't you see how important it is that I get to meet him?"

"And why is that?"

"He's the only one who can give me any answers!" Donna exclaimed, her exasperation growing.

"About your friend, you mean."

Donna sighed deeply. The man was testing her patience further than the police had. "Yes, Father, I told you—"

"Yes, yes," he said impatiently. "You told me all about your friend. But you also told me that she had written to you and that she was apparently fine when she wrote."

Donna stared at him incredulously. She shook her head. "Is it New Yorkers, Father? Or is it just me? How could someone not be concerned under the circumstances?"

"Just what do you want to know, Ms. Miro?"

"That Lorna is all right!"

She was almost shouting. No, there was no "almost" to it. She *was* shouting. She felt as if she had left planet Earth and had come across a strange alien who spoke English, but didn't really comprehend the language.

"What if I assured you that your friend was fine?"

Donna stared at him tensely, her fingers knotting around each other. "Father, I'm sorry, but I'm not really sure I can trust anything that you say. You won't even answer a simple question with a yes or a no!"

He laughed suddenly. "Ms. Miro, I'm not terribly sure that I can trust you. And it isn't my right to trust you, really."

"Oh, Lord!" Donna moaned. "You make no sense!"

"Sorry."

"Is that all that you can say? Father, please! Do you or do you not know Andrew McKennon?"

Ignoring her question, he countered, "What would make you happy, Ms. Miro?"

"Father, I would be happy if I could see Lorna."

"Ah . . ." he murmured. "Of course."

Donna ignored the skepticism in his voice and stared straight at the flames. She had to remain cool and calm and not give way to his piercing eyes and manner. She was beginning to feel that New York was peopled entirely by lunatics. And you had to deal with lunatics very carefully.

"Ms. Miro, you have to realize that I don't know you from Adam."

"What?" Donna gasped.

"Precisely what I said." The priest laughed. "You're asking me questions but I know nothing about you. You're a total stranger to me."

"Father, one of us is totally insane."

He chuckled—a husky sound like smooth velvet that made her very uneasy. "Not insane, Ms. Miro. I'd say we're just skirting around one another carefully."

"Are we?"

"Yes."

"Well, could you skirt around a little less carefully then? Do I look dangerous, Father? You just rescued me from a mugger, so it seems unlikely that I could cause anyone harm."

"Oh, Ms. Miro, I get the impression that you could be very dangerous. In many ways."

His words didn't make sense but his eyes did. She realized that he had assessed her fully as a woman and decided that he hadn't found her lacking. What kind of a priest was this man?

Donna blinked uneasily, drawing her eyes from his unnerving green and gold stare. She stupidly began to notice little things about the room. It was a pleasant room, extremely comfortable with the overstuffed sofa, light marble hearth, and carved oak desk. She noted that ferns and vines climbed and scurried from attractive wicker planters about the rosewood bookshelves that boasted a wide variety of reading material—nonecclesiastical. In fact, there was nothing in particular in the room to indicate that the man was a priest at all.

"Ms. Miro," he began again, his tone changing to one that was strictly business, "I can't tell you anything until—" He broke off suddenly as there was a tap at the door and called out, "Come in, Mary."

Mary bustled back into the room with a tea cart, the top tier carrying a beautifully etched silver tea service and lovely bone-china cups while the lower tier carried a plain yellow bucket. "First things first!" Mary commanded with a smile. "Luke, why don't you serve your guest some tea while I see to her ankle."

Luke complied with no comment. "Cream, sugar, lemon?"

"Just plain, thanks—oh!"

Donna gasped as Mary took a no-nonsense hold of her foot. "Father's right, Miss Miro—nothing here but a mild sprain."

28

Donna heard her shoe make a soft clunking sound as it hit the carpet. "Let's get your stocking off now. . . ."

Mary waited expectantly. Donna again felt herself turn an absurd shade of red. Why couldn't she have been rescued by a nice white-haired priest with a rotund potbelly? Why this man who was once more watching her with amusement-laden eyes that somehow portrayed a sensuality that made heat rip along her spine?

"Come, come, now . . . Donna! We must get this ankle into the hot water—" Mary broke off abruptly, seeing the flush on Donna's cheeks and the electricity that seemed to spark between Luke's devilish gold and her crystal-blue eyes. She laughed delightedly. "I'm so sorry! Luke, step out of the room, please. You're embarrassing the lady!"

Luke smiled, then obligingly left the room. Mary discreetly joined him.

Donna hurriedly ripped off her remaining shoe and her pantyhose, watching the door all the while and berating herself for doing it. He wasn't going to come barging back into the room.

"Miss Miro?" Mary called, tapping on the door lightly.

"All set," Donna returned with a breath of relief.

A second later her ankle was feeling nicely soothed, and Mary was leaning with stern instructions that Donna keep the ankle soaking for at least twenty minutes. Donna was totally taken off guard as the devastating priest brought two cups of tea, handed her one, and sat comfortably beside her on the sofa.

"Well . . . tell me more about yourself," he urged her in a noncommittal tone.

Donna busied herself with her tea, trying to ignore the ruggedly masculine, scintillating scent of his aftershave. She felt that if he touched her again she would shoot through the ceiling with the sear of his magnetic heat.

He was an extremely attractive man, but she was at a loss to understand the intensity of her reactions to him. She tended to be wary of strangers—men in particular—and she had never felt such a physical attraction before. She sipped her tea quickly, silently praying, God, make me stop this! But the feelings stayed with her—and so did the guilt and embarrassment. She had to pull herself together quickly. She couldn't afford to spend a minute dwelling on her strange reactions. Each nuance of his rich voice warned her that he could be a formidable foe.

"You already know my name," she said irritably, now watching the steam that rose above her cup. "I live outside of Worcester, Mass. I'm twenty-eight years old. I graduated from Boston U. with honors. You can check on any of the information I've given you. I'm completely legit, Father, which I'm beginning to think you're not."

Donna heard the flick of a lighter. She turned back to the priest. He had lit a cigarette and was staring idly at the smoke as it whirled into the air. He spoke without glancing her way. "I'm sorry, Ms. Miro. It's just as I've told you. I don't really have the right to tell you anything."

Donna felt every muscle within her body tense. "Why not? What is the great mystery here?"

The golden eyes lit upon her, uncomfortably probing and knowing. He didn't reply.

"There is something very wrong, isn't there?"

He shrugged. "Very wrong? I don't know. I'm not God."

"You might have fooled me," Donna muttered beneath her breath.

"I'm flattered."

How had she wound up playing this absurd battle of wits with a sarcastic priest?

"Just how well do you know Andrew McKennon, Father?"

If she had expected a reaction from her volatile demand, she was to be sadly disappointed. She received another of his subtle shrugs—yet the invasion of his golden eyes was far from subtle.

"Fairly well. He's one of my parishioners."

"Oh," Donna murmured, shielding her eyes with the length of her lashes. A little, inexplicable tremor shook her but she forced herself to look guilelessly into his eyes. "Then you *can* introduce me to him—take me to him. He shouldn't be terribly surprised to see me."

He studied her a long while, his gaze unfathomably raking over her ragged form with no apology. "I'm afraid that it's not quite that easy, Ms. Miro," he said politely.

"How difficult can it be?" Donna demanded, annoyance hiding the fear his question had sent racing through her. Just who or what was Andrew McKennon that this priest was protecting him? "I can't leave New York without meeting McKennon! If you decide not to help me, I'll find another way." She twisted to him, deciding to add a note of entreating charm. "Father, please help me . . ."

Donna's voice trailed off suddenly as she realized that as she had turned, she had placed her hands on his knees. She could feel hard sinewed muscle beneath the black cloth and, again, a heat that was magnetic. She raised her eyes from her hands to his only to feel a new surge of confusion when she found his brow cocked mockingly and his golden eyes glittering again with both amusement and appreciation.

She withdrew her hands as if she had touched fire, which perhaps she had indeed. What the hell was he, devil or angel?

He allowed a smile to filter across his sensuous mouth at her reaction. "I'm afraid it sounds as if you dislike Andrew—and you don't even know him."

Donna stiffened. "I don't dislike him, Father." That was true. How could you hate a mystery man? She could only fear what he might be, or what he might be doing to her friend. She tried to shrug noncommittally. "As you said, I don't know him. I'm merely afraid. For Lorna. Something could happen to her . . . might have al*ready* happened to her. Oh, for God's sake, Father, can't you see that I'm simply concerned! She could be in real danger, she could die, and young women in their twenties shouldn't die!"

"No," he returned, and there was a dry, bitter twist to his deceptively light tone. "Young women in their twenties shouldn't die."

They were both abruptly silent, the silence increasing the tension that was making Donna feel as if she were strung wire.

She sighed suddenly, feeling her entire night had been a ridiculously disturbing ordeal. She constantly felt as if she wanted to reach out and shake him—and then crush him to her. The deadly allure was there. Since the rather dismal end of her own marriage, she had dated a number of attractive men, but never felt the slightest appeal. And now she was sitting there, feeling sensual, totally electric, tension was bidding her to reach out and touch and immerse herself in a man she also wanted to bind to a stake and set afire with a blaze to quench that devil fire in his eyes.

31

And, God help her, he was a priest, and God probably didn't help people who wanted to burn priests.

"Father," she said stiffly. "It's obvious that I've wasted a great deal of time for us both. If you'll just call me a cab—"

Donna barely believed his next words as he interrupted her. "Don't be so hasty. I'll help you, Ms. Miro."

"What?"

"I said that I'd help you."

"Oh, thank you—"

"Don't thank me yet, because I can't promise anything. And if you want my help, you're going to have to agree to a deal."

"A deal?"

"Umm," he murmured, his eyes teasing, but also deadly serious. "The kind signed in blood."

"Sounds like a pact with the devil."

"Does it?"

"And you're supposed to be a priest."

"I am a priest, Ms. Miro. Well, do you want my help or not?"

Donna hesitated, wondering what she was getting into. Then she sighed impatiently, thinking that she should really be running as far from this man as she could get.

"Let's hear about this deal, Father," she murmured.

CHAPTER THREE

"I will help you to find Andrew. I think you should meet him. I can understand that you feel you must assure yourself that your friend is all right, but I don't think that you can see Lorna. And you've stumbled into something that you shouldn't have."

"Stumbled into—"

"Never mind. Forget I said that."

"Forget! How—"

"Because it's the only way that I'll help you. But this is the deal. You keep your mouth shut. You stop driving the police crazy, and you stop searching for Andrew McKennon."

"I can't do that! You just said that something was very wrong. That I'd stumbled into something! And now you're asking me to pretend that none of this exists—"

"No, I'm asking you to keep your mouth shut. But I'm beginning to wonder," he added dryly, "if you're capable of doing that."

"Do you know, Father, you've been giving me comments just like that ever since I found you!" Donna protested.

"I believe I found you, Ms. Miro," he retorted politely.

"Point well taken," Donna acknowledged. "I meet you and discover that you do know this man that no one else has ever heard of. But I shouldn't even be asking about a friend who disappeared. I'm supposed to forget all about it. I don't trust you. But you're going to help me. *If* I can learn to keep my mouth shut."

"In a nutshell, Ms. Miro."

"But I don't know a thing about this McKennon! And everything that happened to Lorna must have started with him!"

"Ms. Miro, I feel I should warn you now that Andrew Mc-

Kennon is more than a parishioner. He is a . . . friend of mine. More than a friend. And if I'd done what I should have done, I would have denied that I knew him. Andrew has to decide what to tell you now, do you understand? I'm going on faith myself right now, Ms. Miro. I have to trust you to be discreet. I shouldn't be doing this at all."

"Then why did you say you would help me? Why did you allow me to go on—"

He stood abruptly, walking to the deep-maroon drapes and pulling them aside. Night had come to Manhattan, but gentle light from the streetlights warmed the tree-lined block in a soft glow. The priest stared out at the trees with their beautiful decking of fall colors for a moment before he turned and sat in the chair behind the oak desk. Then he spoke. "I allowed you to continue because I wanted to hear if you understood me. And I can only repeat that I'll help you find Andrew. But I'd deny a thousand times over that he existed if you started pressing this thing."

Donna's fingers tensed in her lap but she bit back anything she might have to say. Fine. All she wanted to do was find McKennon and then she would take it from there. She'd promise to keep quiet and then do anything that she could to find out where Lorna was. She had to. She had to make Lorna her main concern—even if it meant giving a promise that was a lie to a priest. There was something going on, and for all she knew, this particular priest could be deeply involved in . . . whatever it was.

Could he really be a priest? she wondered for the thousandth time? None of it fit, none of it made sense. But it would have been impossible to plan it all: Mary and the home and the very priestly white collar. And it had been dark, but she was certain that she had seen the steeple of a church just down the street. . . .

Donna started, realizing that the priest was watching her, amusement still touching his features, even though he appeared to be in deep thought. Had he known what she was thinking? Heaven forbid. How could she? She had grown up with such a very, very Catholic family! Yes, that was true, but, she reminded herself, the friars who had conducted the Inquisition had been religious men.

"Ms. Miro, are you quite all right?" he queried her suddenly.

"Fine, thank you. But would you mind telling me what you're doing?"

"Not at all. I'm thinking."

He drummed his fingers on the desk and started speaking again, slowly, as if he carefully weighed each word. "Andrew is not always an easy man to find, Ms. Miro. I haven't the right to explain to you why that is. If you want my help, you're going to have to trust me."

"But why—"

"Questions already!" he reproached her.

"Father, you make less sense by the moment."

"Nothing is going to make sense to you, but I can't change that. It's going to have to be part of the deal."

"Ah, yes! The deal," Donna murmured with annoyance.

"Yes, the deal." He raised a dark brow high, as if questioning her integrity. "It begins right now. And it encompasses only this, Ms. Miro. You're going to have to put your faith in me. Absolutely no questions asked. No matter what you think, see, or hear, you're going to have to believe me when I tell you that Andrew McKennon is a good man—and that what I'm asking of you is for your own good."

"You want me to go by blind faith?" Donna asked incredulously. "In you?" Was he asking her the ridiculous, or could it be true that Andrew McKennon was not a bad or evil man? That the priest couldn't—for reasons unknown to her—say more, but that he was really trying to give her an emotional assurance?

Father Luke smiled. Faint lines of laughter crinkled about his eyes, giving them a mocking and devilish glow. He lifted his hands, as if to heaven. "Blind faith? In me. Yes, I suppose I do want you to go by blind faith. I've gotten quite accustomed to doing it myself, you see." The laughter faded from his handsome features. "It's the only way that I will help you, Ms. Miro."

Suddenly Donna found that she couldn't meet his eyes—eyes that raked over her with both a peculiar appreciation and a searing that seemed to touch her soul. She felt absurdly stripped by that gaze; as if she had been taken down to naked flesh—and naked motive. He was a very strange man. Compelling, fright-

35

ening. She began to feel that she might have been safer in the hands of the mugger. There was about him a sense of energy, and of danger, and of sexuality. He truly had no right to be a priest.

"Well?" He demanded suddenly.

Donna paused a minute, wondering what purgatory awaited those who purposely lied to priests. She swept her lashes over her cheeks. Andrew McKennon was impossible to find. She had hired a private detective, who had gotten nowhere. She had tried the police, and they had almost thrown her out the door. She had tried the streets and fared even worse.

"Blind faith, Father. All that I want to do is meet McKennon for myself and get some kind of real assurance that Lorna is all right."

She watched as he suddenly frowned, then drummed his fingers on the desk for a moment and picked up the telephone. After a second a smile touched his features, making Donna once more acutely aware of his devilish, ruggedly male good looks.

"Tricia? Ummm . . . it's Luke. Fine . . . fine . . . thanks. Listen, I'd like to see you as soon as possible. It's about Andrew."

Apparently "Tricia" had a few things to say about the reason for his call. Not angry things; just worried things. The next thing Donna heard was the priest reassuring the woman. "You know that if I didn't really believe that what I was doing was okay, I wouldn't be doing it."

More conversation. Then: "Trust me. Andrew would."

Donna waited tensely as the woman replied. The priest's golden eyes abruptly turned her way. "Where are you staying?" he demanded.

"The Plaza," Donna replied quickly.

His gaze swept swiftly over her body and his ever-subtle grin touched his lips. "Where else?" he murmured, as if directing his question with a certain amused exasperation to the divinity above.

Donna ground her teeth together to keep from snapping out a reply. It didn't matter. The priest was speaking to Tricia— whoever she was—again.

"How about the Oak Room at the Plaza? Ummm . . . bet-

36

ter give us an hour. I don't want to give anyone a scare in my raven weeds and I'm certain Ms. Miro is going to want to change. Eight sounds perfect." He glanced at Donna and suddenly laughed. "Don't worry about the expense, Tricia. The lady I'm bringing with me will pick up the tab." He laughed again, then closed with "Thanks, Tricia."

He hung up the phone and stood quickly. "Excuse me, will you, Ms. Miro? I'll be back down directly."

"Wait a minute," Donna demanded, but he ignored her. His long, sure strides took him out of the room before he could reply. Donna sat fuming for a moment with her foot still soaking, wondering just what she was getting herself into. She had the strangest feeling she was playing with fire.

She stood with sudden vehemence, wincing as she placed weight upon the still-soaking foot. It didn't matter! she thought angrily. She owed it to Lorna to find out what was going on, if she really was all right.

Donna winced and glanced down at her foot. The ankle wasn't half so painful as it had been. She grimaced, remembering what might have happened to her if the disturbing priest hadn't come upon her. She was grateful to him, she reluctantly admitted to herself as she tentatively removed her foot and shook it slightly so that water would drip off. But, hell, what a messy situation she had literally fallen into. She didn't even know what was going on.

Grimacing slightly and looking about guiltily, Donna placed her still-damp foot on the thick Oriental carpeting. Her foot seemed to take her weight if she was very careful.

Silently fuming, she gazed about the room. This time she noted the mounted deer head above the mantel and the gun rack in its handsome wood case against the far wall. The man was incredible.

He swore like a truck driver, cuffed would-be thiefs, hunted and had the closest damn thing to bedroom eyes she'd ever seen. Oh, why had God put this man in her path?—and a priest, no less.

Donna stopped muttering to herself as her idle hobbling brought her to his desk. The piece was as comfortably tasteful, austere, uncluttered, and as simple as the rest of the room. As the man? Surely, no. He was more like a walking powder keg but then, he could also hide his emotions. He released his anger only when it served his purpose. He was capable of raw violence, but that violence was very purposely controlled. She should know. He had used it to rescue her from a terrifying experience.

Cautiously she moved to the bookcase. Ah! At least there was a Bible in it. *Confessions of Saint Augustine.* A number of things by Andrew Greeley. Why not?

Donna kept combing the bookcases. There were novels by Robert Ludlum, Sidney Sheldon, and a number of other contemporary writers. A copy of *Moby Dick,* Beckett, and a bound collection of Shakespeare, Plays by Molière. . . .

There were also a number of books on the occult: *Witchcraft Today. Understanding ESP. A History of Magic/White and Black.* And then there were *The Psychosis of the Criminal Mind, In the Eyes of the Strangler,* and *An Analysis of One Murderer.*

There were more books. A lot of law books. Books on architecture, on history, and a number of "do-it-yourself" books.

But it was the books on the occult and "criminal minds" that made her shiver. Besides the obvious, she felt that the priest was a mystery, that there was something about himself that he kept hidden.

Maybe she should be getting the hell out of there—going as far away as she could! She didn't know anything about him at all, much less about anything that he might be hiding!

She closed her eyes. She couldn't leave. She had to help Lorna. Yet at what cost to herself?

She started her half-limping, idle wandering about the room once again. And then her thoughts took on a sudden change as her eyes fell on a picture on his desk in a plain brass frame. The picture was of a young woman who had a face with a classic beauty in fine oval features and more. The photographer had caught her animation, the sparkle of dark amber eyes, even the whirling flow of golden blond hair.

As Donna pondered the small portrait, Mary suddenly swept back into the room, holding a bandage. "Donna! You shouldn't be standing on that foot!"

Donna swallowed guiltily. "I-I'm sorry, Mary. But I had to

try it—and it is so much better. Thank you. And I am so sorry if I soaked your carpet—"

"The carpet will dry! Not to worry about a thing like that! But you get off that foot now and stand only when you have to."

Donna started to hobble obediently back to the sofa, but she couldn't resist one backward glance to the portrait. Mary saw the direction of her eyes and smiled sadly. "April was a lovely, lovely girl, don't you think? Ahhh . . . Luke was so in love with her. And she with him. But . . . the good Lord takes us all when he will."

Donna was glad she had reached the sofa, for she would have fallen to the floor without it. As it was, it was all she could do to hold back a gasp of shock. God grant it, "Father" Luke gave the appearance of being an extremely healthy and virile man; he had eyes like the devil himself and exuded strength and vibrant sensuality—but the man was a priest!

How could his kindly housekeeper speak so nonchalantly about his loving a woman? Unless, of course, this April had been his wife before he became a priest? Her shock receded then, and she recalled with a sympathetic poignancy his words: "No, young women in their twenties shouldn't die," words that had held a note of bitter pain.

She swallowed quickly, attempting a small smile as Mary's eyes turned to hers. She couldn't resist further temptation.

"Who . . . uh . . . was she, Mary?"

"Why, April, Donna? Ahh . . . and just like a spring day, she was. So sweet, and gentle. And—"

"Mary!"

The housekeeper's name was called sharply from the doorway. Neither woman had noticed that the door had swung open —or that the priest had returned to tower within it. Except that he didn't look like a priest any more. He was still in black, but now he wore a light-blue open-neck knit shirt beneath a casual black leather jacket.

He might have just stepped from a page of *The New Yorker*. Elegantly casual man about town, the type who drove a Ferrari and had a dozen blondes practically purring as they lounged about him in sleek poses.

"Excuse me"—his tone gentled and he offered a brief smile to his housekeeper—"but we have to hurry, Mary." His glance turned sharply to Donna. "Ms. Miro? I'm afraid we'll have to go now if we're to make our appointment. I do think you need time to make yourself a little more presentable."

Donna automatically placed a hand on the escaping tendrils of her hair. She was a disaster. No pantyhose, no shoes. One foot soaked and still dripping. Clothing dirtied and crumpled, hair a disheveled mass. And she was going to the Oak Room with a man who was definitely the most striking individual she had ever encountered.

"Luke! Give the girl a minute!" Mary said firmly. She smiled warmly at Donna. "Give me just a second. I'll get an Ace bandage wrapped around your ankle and it'll be as good as new!"

Mary gave her employer a chastising stare as she bent down and took Donna's ankle in her hand. Donna had to grit her teeth for a minute as Mary wrapped the bandage around her ankle, but once it was in place and her shoes were back on, she found that she could stand with little discomfort.

"Ms. Miro? Are we ready yet?" The priest queried her as she balanced a bit doubtfully.

"I . . . uh . . . yes! I'm ready. Mary, thank you so much for everything."

"Nothing at all, dear. Nothing at all. And I'm so sure we'll be seeing more of one another!"

Donna had no reply. She hobbled quickly to the doorway where she stared up at . . . the man. The flecks of molten gold and green in eyes seemed to fuse to the shade of fire as he returned her scrutiny with humor. He offered her his arm and she had little choice but to accept. His touch seemed to burn with the heat of his eyes. It rippled through her. It made her more acutely aware of being a woman than she had ever known possible.

"Come on, Ms. Miro, our chariot is waiting."

She swallowed and lowered her lashes and hurried along beside him. Whomever, or whatever, Father Luke actually was, the effect he had upon her was definitely sinful.

CHAPTER FOUR

In the dimness of the cab Donna could see a reflected gleam in the golden eyes that seemed ever more satanically appealing in the neon glow of night. Something about him just wasn't right.

Donna drew her gaze from him to stare out the window, thankful to recognize the area of Central Park South. A hansom cab pulled by a large bay gelding clattered by as they stopped at a traffic light. Donna jerked back around to face the man beside her. The whole situation was driving her crazy.

"Are you Catholic?" she demanded.

He glanced her way with lazy, heavy lidded eyes. "Do you know the meaning of the word, Ms. Miro?"

"Of course: 'universal.' "

"Then I suppose I can certainly say I'm catholic."

"What kind of an answer is that?" she demanded. The taxi seemed terribly small.

"The best you're going to get, Ms. Miro. Except that I'll hasten to assure you I didn't create a charade of my life simply for your benefit this evening."

So he was a priest. She felt a little doomed because she was falling beneath the spell of his fascination and was attracted to a man who had dedicated his life to a different calling. How did she deal with him?

A baseball bat would have been nice. Right across the back of his head. She wanted to label him as arrogant—but she couldn't, not quite. He was quick to parry her thrusts, yet his voice always carried a low note of humor that wasn't cruel, merely amused, as if he were clearly aware of her dilemma and enjoying it. Arrogant . . . no, not exactly. He was an assured man, confident in himself . . . electrically vital. . . .

Like Mark. Donna's mouth twisted into a sad smile as she thought of the man who had once been her husband. Mark could walk into a room and charm everyone. His eyes carried that bold flash of appreciation and challenge. So dynamic. Lorna had told her once that Mark had been too dynamic and that it would be hard for her to fall in love again because she would have to find a man more dynamic to make her forget him.

This man was dynamic. He made her forget everything, even the fact that he was a priest. And the attraction was still there—perhaps worse in the cab—a chemistry that was blinding. An undeniable, overpowering instinct to go to him.

She was floundering in quicksand. And yet, if he were any other man, she would have been certain that he was as riddled by the magical yet natural beguilement as she. Even when she wanted to slap him she wanted to feel the strong, clean-shaven contours of his jaw. . . .

"My turn," he said suddenly.

"For what?" Donna asked, meeting his eyes uneasily.

"Are you . . . Roman Catholic, Ms. Miro?"

In the near future, she would regret that she gave little notice to his emphasis on the adjective "Roman." But she was tired and sore, confused, angry—and disturbed by his very unpriestly presence. She answered him flippantly. "Me? Of course, Father. An Italian girl from Shrewesbury Street? They consider us to be very, very Catholic!"

Donna noticed her fingers were shaking as she drew further against her side of the cab. The distance didn't help. She stilled her fingers with strength of will and began a new line of questioning.

"Who is this Tricia? Why are we meeting her?"

"She is a friend of mine—and she keeps in touch with Andrew more closely than I do."

Donna was unable to query him further since the cab pulled in front of the entrance to the Plaza. Again she attempted to pay—and again she was impatiently brushed aside.

The large, beautiful lobby of the hotel was brimming with people. Saturday night, Donna thought dryly. Masses of people were descending for a night out on the town, bedecked in all sorts of regalia for the theater or dinner or dancing. Donna threaded her way toward the elevators, trying to talk over her shoulder.

"Please go on in to the Oak Room. I'll meet you as soon as I'm able."

"Oh, I wouldn't dream of leaving you, Ms. Miro. You could trip somewhere on that ankle. Or you could get your directions backward and spend the next twenty-four hours looking for the Oak Room."

She wanted to argue with him—she certainly didn't want him coming to her room—but it was impossible to argue in the crowd as he calmly ushered her along by the elbow. Once inside the crowded elevator, she gave up with a sigh, wondering then just how she had left her room. She had a habit of really spreading out—leaving hair spray on the nightstand, bobby pins all over the sink, and her toiletries from one end of a bureau to another. Face it, she had a habit of being disorganized, and also —when she was pressed for time—of leaving discarded clothing wherever it had fallen.

"What floor, Ms. Miro?"

Donna answered him brusquely, once again wondering about the state of her room. She could recall nothing—except that she had been in a hurry to get going.

Too soon they were walking down the hall and she was fumbling in the shoulder bag for the little code card that was her key. It was galling to realize that she couldn't even function properly when he stood beside her. For several years she had considered herself immune to attractive males and now. . . .

But it wasn't just her, she thought defensively. He had drawn the eyes of every female in both elevator and lobby. Almost everyone, she corrected herself. He was a riveting man. Strength of will? she wondered. Or perhaps the self-assurance that was purposeful?

"May I help?"

She wasn't even managing to slip the little card into the door.

He took the initiative without reply and a second later they were entering the room.

Donna was loath to turn on the light but equally loath to be alone with him in the darkness. She quickly hit the switch.

The beds were made, but that was about it. She had only been in New York a day and already she had a clutter of shoes next to the dresser, jackets thrown over one bed and a chair, and an assortment of toiletries strewn across the dresser.

Latent childhood rebellion, she thought briefly. Her mother was the perfect Italian housewife to the core—to this day she studiously ironed the permanent-pressed sheets and her father's boxer shorts.

"Uh . . . I'll just be a second," Donna murmured nervously as she headed for the closet, trying to kick her shoe assortment beneath the dresser unobtrusively. "Just make yourself comfortable—"

She broke off, glad that she was facing the clothing she had hung up. Make yourself comfortable! Surely that wasn't the right thing to say when a priest stood in one's hotel room.

She grabbed a sleek navy cocktail dress and backed out of the closet. He was about to sit in the one large fanback chair that faced the window overlooking the park when he paused. Donna frowned, but he straightened with a smile, dangling a pair of red lace panties from his forefinger. "Will you be needing these?" he inquired with bland innocence.

Donna pursed her lips and stomped to retrieve her garment —causing her ankle to buckle with pain. He was quick to rescue her with a firm grip on the arm, but Donna felt little gratitude.

"Thank you," she muttered, snatching them from him and straightening herself quickly. She made a quick escape into the bathroom, the husky sound of his chuckle following her.

She leaned against the closed door for a moment, trying to slow the erratic beating of her heart and the great gulps she was taking in for air.

"He can't be a priest!" she mouthed.

She stumbled over her own clothing as she tried to change, but she still managed to ger her clothes on quickly. She gave up on trying to repin her hair and simply brushed it and allowed it to hang loose. No time for makeup repair. And she had forgotten to burrow through a drawer for a new pair of stockings. . . . Damn.

Drawing a deep breath, she exited the bathroom in her bare feet. He was watching her every movement, sitting comfortably with an ankle crossed over a knee, his dark head relaxed against the chair, his fingers idly strumming its arms.

44

"Tell me, Ms. Miro, how does a girl from Shrewesbury Street wind up at the Plaza?"

Donna paused and straightened from the drawer she had been searching to face him through the mirror. "You tell me first, Father Luke, how a priest happens to wear custom clothing?"

He smiled nonchalantly. "I have two sisters, Ms. Miro. They're both fond of lavishing gifts on me at Christmas."

It didn't ring exactly true. But then it didn't sound like a lie either.

Donna found a pair of stockings and slammed the drawer shut.

"Okay, fair enough. We made money in the olive-oil business," she said, continuing quickly with a defense mechanism that had become mechanical since her college days. "The legit olive-oil business. Being of Italian descent does not automatically make one a member of organized crime."

He lifted his dark eyebrows high with humor. "My dear Ms. Miro, I would have never assumed such a thing."

Donna flushed slightly. "I'm sorry. I got tired of the teasing at Boston U. when everyone asked if I could get a hit man for a certain professor when exams were coming up."

"No one likes to be stereotyped, Ms. Miro."

There was a calm authority to his gentle words that sent her flying back to the bathroom in confusion. What was going on here? she screamed inwardly as she stepped into the fresh stockings. She had to get away from this man—but he was her only link to Andrew McKennon and, therefore, to Lorna.

She closed her eyes for a moment, fighting the pain that could still touch her so easily. She had to find Lorna. Or did she? Maybe she should have stayed out of it . . .

No. She exhaled a deep sigh. She had thought it over again and again. Lorna was as close to her as her brothers and sisters. Maybe closer. They had been friends since they had been five years old. She couldn't take a chance that everything was all right. She had to know. If something were to happen to Lorna, she would never forgive herself for not getting involved.

Okay, so she was involved. And being involved had cast her into the company of a priest who was making her feel as if her muscles had become wet cement and her bones had turned to

45

jelly. Who teased her, confused her, frightened her, excited her, and made her fear for her soul.

Donna straightened and surveyed her reflection in the mirror. Her dress was simple and concealing, yet nicely sophisticated. She was twenty-eight, adjusted to the world around her, sure of her views and goals, and comfortable in her relationships with family and friends. She was not going to allow herself to appear unnerved.

She tilted her chin slightly and flicked her long hair behind her shoulder. She was ready.

This time she strode out of the bathroom with a calm assurance, pausing only to transfer a few things from her shoulder bag to a smaller evening purse. She didn't glance at the man whose eyes she could feel like brands on her back until her task was complete. Then she turned and sauntered as best she could, with her ankle still weak, for the door, gripping the handle and swinging it open. "Shall we go—Father?"

He stood and strode toward her. "Certainly, Ms. Miro."

Despite her resolve, she lowered her eyes as he reached her. "Could you please quit that?"

"What is it you wish me to quit?" he inquired softly.

She wondered bitterly how even the husky depths of his voice could touch her like a sensual caress. Somehow she raised her eyes to his. "My name is Donna."

"Donna," he said agreeably, inclining his head with a slight grin curved into his handsome features.

"I wish I knew," she murmured, dismayed to hear that her own voice was husky, "how I should really be addressing *you.*"

He chuckled, breaking the spell that had seemed to bind them to the doorway as he slipped an arm through hers to lead her out and down the hallway. "My name, Donna, is Lucian Trudeau. Father Trudeau, if you will. Or Father Luke."

"I'm really not terribly sure I can call you Father Luke," Donna exhaled on a whisper of air.

She felt the bend of his head to her ear, a touch of velvet that streaked like fire along her spine as he spoke softly. "Then don't, Donna. Most people merely call me Luke."

The elevator door parted. This time they were alone as they moved into the cubicle. Donna wanted to shrink into a corner. She forced herself to remain calm and still.

But she almost screamed when he reached out to lightly lift the heavy length of her hair from her shoulder. She could feel the brush of his fingers with every nerve within her. That slight contact made waves of trembling heat sweep through her.

"Your hair is one of the most beautiful, unique shades I've ever seen," he told her softly.

He wasn't doing anything. Nothing intimate. The gesture was not in the least a come-on—he still stood a foot away from her —and yet it swamped her senses far more thoroughly than the most passionate kiss she had ever received.

"Just your usual dark Italian brown," she replied, trying to laugh. But her voice trembled. It was throaty and husky. She stared ahead at the doors, praying they would open. "But thank you," she murmured.

He released her hair. His knuckles once more brushed her cheek, but his eyes were locked with hers. Somehow burning, somehow soft. That strange green and gold. Compelling, captivating.

They touched her and warmed her. And for a long while, she returned that stare. And all she could think was that she liked him very much. It was as if he searched for something in her and found it. They barely knew one another, but instinct told Donna that there was something right between them. The chemistry that made a certain man right for a certain woman. He was the type of man with whom she could very easily fall in love. . . .

He was a priest, he was a priest, he was a priest. . . .

She forced herself to tear her eyes from his, and she repeated the words over and over again to convince herself that they were true.

It was crazy, it was all crazy. The night had pitched her into things she didn't understand, and she had made some kind of an absurd promise to go along with it.

It seemed that they had been in the elevator a ridiculously long time. They had to reach the lobby. Soon. She couldn't stand being so close to him when they were so confined. She felt as if she were metal and he were a magnet, pulling her irrevocably to him.

He was the priest; Donna was the one who began to pray.

She prayed desperately that the elevator would reach the lobby.

Her prayer was answered and the doors slid silently open.

CHAPTER FIVE

They didn't speak as they made their way through the lobby with its gracious store displays of clothing and jewels to the Oak Room. Donna was not surprised when the maitre d' appeared to know her escort well. Nothing much about the strange priest would have surprised her anymore. They were led to a corner table with a snowy white cloth, where a very pretty young brunette awaited them. She stood as they reached the table, smiling quickly at Donna and then offering Luke an unabashed hug and kiss.

Donna stood staring at the tablecloth as the two greeted one another. Luke—Father Luke—returned the brunette's kiss with much more than what Donna would have termed "fatherly" appreciation.

He pulled out Donna's chair, but his attention was still on the other woman. "Tricia, you look wonderful. That dress has to be the sexiest damn thing I've ever seen."

Tricia blushed prettily. "Luke . . . you're the world's worst tease. As if you didn't already have the female half of Manhattan panting at your feet." Her attention turned a bit warily to Donna, who was having great difficulty maintaining a noncommittal expression after the exchange she had just witnessed.

"Tricia," Luke said, "this is Donna Miro. She is a good friend of Lorna's and she's trying to locate Andrew."

"Oh," Tricia murmured, then she smiled. "It's very nice to meet you, Donna. Especially if you're a friend of Lorna's."

"Thank you," Donna murmured, still wondering just exactly who Tricia was and attempting to hide the anger growing within her as she realized Luke not only knew Andrew but obviously knew Lorna as well.

"It's a pleasure to meet you, Tricia, and I can't tell you how much it will mean to me to find Andrew McKennon—and Lorna."

Tricia shot Luke an accusing stare. He shrugged and told Donna, "I never promised that you'd see Lorna."

"But why . . . ?"

His eyes met hers. No questions, they warned. Her words faded in her throat.

"I don't know exactly what Luke has told you, Miss Miro." Tricia, flushing slightly, looked uncomfortable, "I'm sure this is very confusing to you, but it's an extremely delicate situation." She smiled uncertainly as their waiter arrived. Luke automatically ordered wine for Tricia and a scotch for himself, then lifted his brows at Donna.

"I don't think I care for a drink."

Luke chuckled. "That's strange, Donna. You look as if you could happily indulge in a few doubles."

She couldn't prevent her look from being venomous at his assessment. "I think I will also have a glass of wine then," she told the waiter with her best possible forced smile.

They were given dinner menus and then their very proper waiter hurried away. Tricia leaned across the table to speak to Donna, a puzzled frown furrowing her brow. "I wish you could just believe me when I say that Lorna is fine."

Donna smiled. "I wish that I could believe you too. But I'm afraid I need something more—from someone."

"Well," Tricia murmured, "that will have to be Andrew's decision."

Andrew's decision, Andrew's decision! Donna was tempted to pound on the table and tell them both that the almighty Andrew could rot in hell because she'd just go to the police.

But she'd already tried the police. . . .

"I can't begin to understand all this! You tell me that Lorna is all right but that I can't see her. Please, I'm trying to be patient. I'm searching really hard for some faith but it's getting harder and harder to come by!" Donna said bitterly.

Tricia and Luke exchanged glances. Donna was surprised to see both sorrow and empathy in Tricia's eyes. Luke appeared annoyed.

50

"I told you," he said to Donna lightly, "that you weren't to ask any questions."

"How can I help—"

"Try a little harder for that faith, Ms. Miro. Remember, I did warn you that that was the way it was going to be."

"Okay, then," Donna said, smiling sweetly at Tricia. "What happens now?"

Tricia returned her smile. "Donna, I do understand what you must be going through. Lorna is lucky to have such a friend. I'll do my best to get hold of Andrew. Between Luke and me, one of us should be able to reach him soon. Hopefully, he'll be able to give you all the assurances that you need."

"If I could just talk to Lorna! Please, Tricia, if you would just tell me—"

Tricia stood suddenly, smiling down at both of them. "I'm awfully sorry, Donna, but will you excuse me for just a moment? I have to use the ladies' room and I didn't want to leave while I was still waiting for you."

Luke was already on his feet. "Of course, Tricia. We'll wait for you to get back to order dinner."

"Thanks." She smiled briefly.

They watched her as she skirted tables to exit the room.

"Saved by nature's call, Donna?"

"Saved from what?"

"A breech of faith. You were asking questions again."

Irritably Donna turned her gaze to the striking priest, finding the amused mockery she anticipated lighting the gold in his eyes to a dangerous glitter.

"And what saves you, Father Luke?"

"Saves me?" He hiked a brow in polite inquiry.

"Father, you flirt like a damned pirate. Has that practice been approved by the Pope lately?"

"Hmm . . . not that I know of," he replied, nonplussed. His grin deepened as he dipped his head near hers. "Tricia is a lovely woman. And alas, Ms. Miro, I'm a priest—not a saint."

"Oh, my God!" Donna moaned.

"Please, don't get so possessive with the divinity!"

Donna was sorely tempted to toss her water glass over his head, but he suddenly discarded his light, taunting attitude and sat back in his chair, eyeing her acutely as he drew a cigarette

51

from his jacket pocket and lit it. "So tell me," he demanded, and she felt a little chill as she saw again the man who had so expertly and ruthlessly nailed her attacker to the wall. "Where do we go from here, Donna?"

"What do you mean?"

"I mean that you're going to have to decide to trust someone. I can promise you that if you ask questions in the wrong places, you won't find your friend, but you could seriously jeopardize her situation."

"You know Lorna, don't you?"

"Yes."

"Why didn't you tell me?"

"You never asked me."

"I never asked—" Donna began, then interrupted herself. "Has anyone ever told you that you are an extremely exasperating and infuriating human being?"

He chuckled softly. "Yes, as a matter of fact. My bishop did, just last week. But you didn't need to tell me that you felt that way."

"Really?"

"You are so sadly transparent."

"I have a right to be!" Donna exclaimed. "This whole thing is shrouded in the most absurd secrecy!"

Luke suddenly leaned close to her, and she felt a dangerous tension about him, so much so that it took great willpower to keep from inching away from him.

"Donna, you are treading into very deep water. Watch your step. It's blind faith, or nothing."

Donna didn't have a chance to reply. The waiter came and delivered their drinks, and then Tricia was sliding back into her seat. Luke, once again eyeing Donna with amusement, offered a toast to beautiful women. Grinding down on her teeth, Donna managed to smile and clink glasses with them both.

"Miss Miro," Tricia said with soft-spoken excitement, "I managed to get a call through to Andrew. He couldn't give me a guarantee, but if he can, he'll be at Evening Prayer tomorrow night, and he'll meet you in Luke's rectory right after. He asks, though, that you be discreet."

"Discreet?" Donna murmured, but Tricia's excitement was contagious, and all that Donna could see was a ray of sunlight after stumbling around in pools of darkness. She was going to get to see the mysterious Andrew McKennon!

"I'll be there!" Donna promised.

"It's a five o'clock service."

"Fine. I'd be there at midnight if he wanted! I'll definitely be there at five!"

"Not alone, you won't."

Donna was startled by Luke's harsh interruption. She glanced his way to discover that his jaw was locked at a tense angle and that he was staring peculiarly at Tricia. More peculiar was the fact that Tricia seemed to understand that angry and warning expression.

"I'll tell you what, Miss Miro. I'll come here tomorrow at four to meet you, and we'll go together. Is that all right, Luke?"

He nodded.

Donna stared at him incredulously for a minute. It was true that he had saved her from a mugging—and possibly worse—but that didn't give him the right to run her life as if she were a small child.

"Excuse me, Father," she snapped, "but I am capable of giving a cab driver an address! I might have stumbled into trouble tonight, but I'm too old for a keeper!"

"Donna . . . Miss Miro. . . ." Tricia murmured, distressed by the obvious tension rising between her dinner companions, "I don't mind coming for you at all. There's a reason."

"Is there?"

"Yes," Tricia said hurriedly. Luke was scowling, but she continued anyway. "We've been having a rather nasty rash of robberies here over the past year. The police have been floundering in all their attempts to catch this man—or men. He attacks single women coming and going from churches." She smiled ruefully. "He's a nondenominational thief. I really don't mean that humorously; it's a terrible situation, and a number of people have been hurt. . . ."

She paused suddenly, glancing at Luke. His features seemed to be strained and tense; once again his jaw was twisted and locked. His eyes seemed to burn into Tricia like a golden blaze from hell. Tricia tore her eyes from his and continued. "A number of women have been hurt very badly."

53

"I think I'd be okay in a taxi," Donna said slowly, "but I appreciate your concern."

"I need to go to church anyway," Tricia said.

Donna shrugged, at a loss. "If you really want to, Tricia. I guess it doesn't make much difference." She laughed. "I don't know the address of the church or the rectory anyway."

"Excuse me, ladies," Luke interrupted, "but I think we should order. This is Saturday night—"

"Oh, yes!" Tricia glanced quickly at her watch. "I'll just have time. . . . I have to be to the club by ten."

"You'll make it," Luke assured her. He gazed at Donna, his dark-lashed golden gaze still seeming to be riddled with vast amusement. "Tricia sings in a small club uptown. Perhaps if you stay in New York long enough, you'll accompany me to her show. It's a delightful place. Elegant . . . and very, very intimate."

Donna was dying to snap out that she wouldn't accompany him to a dog fight, but she held back the thought and inclined her head slightly. "I'm hoping not to remain in New York very long, Father. Only long enough to meet with Mr. McKennon."

He smiled, and Donna thought she would never in a thousand years trust such a smile. It was as dangerous as all hell. It touched off a chord within her that was a stimulus so strong it was terrifying.

Donna glanced quickly at her menu. The words blurred before her so she readily accepted Luke's suggestion of the prime rib. As he ordered their meals, Donna turned her attention to the pianist at the rear of the room who played soft ballads. It was a perfect place for dinner, Donna thought. Quiet music so that people could talk, and yet a number of couples were enjoying slow dancing.

"Donna?"

She turned back to Luke, blinking. The subtle smile that belonged on either a pirate or the devil curved his lips and touched his eyes at her startled response.

"Will you join me on the dance floor? Tricia assures me she doesn't mind in the least. It's a slow dance so you can lean against me and your ankle won't have to bear any weight. And it's wrapped well. Come on, Donna."

"No!"

The single word came out in a panicked yelp, which did her little good, because he was drawing her to her feet anyway, and rather than trip over her bad ankle, she was forced to lean on him.

"I do not want to dance!" she grated out as he led her to the floor.

"Yes, you do," he whispered, slipping his arms around her. The entire night—or perhaps God—seemed to be conspiring against her. The music became slow, a song for lovers. Her arms mechanically wound around his neck; her cheek rested against the lapel of his jacket, and for the life of her, she couldn't fight the riot of sensations that filled her. His pleasant, very male scent, the warmth of his body, the strength of his arms. The feel of that scratchy cloth beneath the softness of her cheek. He moved with a slow and easy grace; she felt she could too easily follow him wherever he led. . . .

But he supposedly was a man of God; yet he was playing dark games of secrecy with her. He was hiding something. . . .

"I brought you out here," he whispered, his breath warm as it seemed to caress the lobe of her ear as he ducked his head low, pulling her even closer, "to threaten you."

"Threaten me!" She tried to pull from the strong grasp of his arms.

"Take it easy!" he said. "This is the last time I'm going to ask you to take things at face value."

"Blind faith again? You've got it . . . Luke. Until tomorrow night, at least."

"Good. Because any more questions and your meeting with Andrew will be off."

"I can just go to the police—"

"You're a liar, Donna. You've already been to the police."

"For a priest," Donna grated dryly, "you really are one hell of a pain in the neck. I would really rather not dance any more."

"All right, but during dinner, we talk about New York, sports, movies—or the state of the world. We do not discuss Andrew McKennon. Got it? I'm the one who put Tricia into the middle of this situation, for your benefit. So for my benefit, you're not going to make her miserable."

"Oh, I got it," Donna replied. They had pulled away from

one another and stood facing each other angrily on the dance floor. He lifted a hand and a brow, suggesting that she lead the way back to the table. Donna spun about and felt his hand fall lightly to her waist. A polite touch, a guiding touch. One she resented nevertheless. Resented . . . and felt through to the core of her being.

Tricia was smiling when they reached the table. "That wasn't a long dance!" She laughed.

"My ankle is bothering me a bit," Donna murmured, annoyed that she found herself lowering her lashes over her eyes rather than meeting Luke's speculative and amused gaze.

He pulled out her chair and she sat. As he joined her, he said something to Tricia about a new show he had seen Off-Broadway and they began to talk about the theater.

Dinner was served. Donna barely tasted her food, but what she did taste was good, and thanks to Tricia's pleasant nature, the meal passed quickly. She was sorry when Tricia rose, telling them both to stay seated, that she had to get to work.

Luke rose anyway. "I'll walk you out for a taxi, Tricia—"

"Don't be silly, Luke. There's a doorman on duty! And, oh, about dinner—"

Luke laughed, casting Donna one of his subtly amused and mocking gazes. "Don't worry about dinner, Trish. It's on our delightful olive-oil heiress, Ms. Miro."

Donna managed to smile as Trish voiced her thanks, then ran out, promising to pick her up by four the next day. Luke sat down beside her again, and she met his amused gaze with irritation.

"One day," she promised him, "God will punish you for all this."

"Will he?" Luke laughed. "I'm sure I will deserve my days in purgatory, but not for this."

"Maybe you'll get to rot in hell," Donna said sweetly.

"Maybe. None of us knows for sure."

The check came. Luke kept smiling while Donna signed it, then pushed back her chair and rose.

"Well, Father, I suppose I'll see you at church tomorrow."

"Yes, I suppose you will." He rose and took her elbow.

Donna sighed. "I can get to my room by myself, Father."

"I'm sure you can."

"But I won't?"

"Very perceptive, Donna."

"What does the church think of priests who bribe and threaten the innocent?"

"Are you innocent?"

"Oh, God!" She groaned.

"Come on, I'll see you to your room."

They made the trek to the elevator again and then down the hall to her room in silence. She made no protest when he took the card key and unlocked the door. He pushed it open, turned on the light, and strode into the room, making no excuses as he checked out her closet and bath.

"All clear," he murmured cheerfully.

"Thanks," Donna murmured.

He moved to where she stood in the doorway. In that small space, they were very close. The scent that was male and pleasant came to her again, and it suddenly seemed as if her knees could very easily buckle. She gazed into his eyes with their misted gold and green, and felt a fierce trembling along with the desire to reach out and touch the bronzed texture of his cheek. He was a priest, she tried to remind herself. But the thought wouldn't come; he was a man, one who attracted her more than she had ever thought possible, one who reached out to her, excited her, stirred her . . . touched her. Something happened to her in those moments, something that she would never understand.

The seconds ticked by as they stared at one another. She couldn't seem to move . . . not until he did. His hand came to her waist, slid to her hip, then slowly up her spine until his fingers wound into the hair at her nape. She had no thought to fight him as he tilted her head back, as his free hand slipped around her, bringing her firmly against him. He was hard and warm and wonderful, and she felt the length of his body with her own before she closed her eyes and felt the gentle force of his lips touching her own, urging them apart.

She felt his tongue, moving, caressing, exploring more and more deeply, as probing as his eyes, touching her soul, exciting her, making her feel faint. She clung to him, she lifted her fingertips to his cheeks. Freshly shaved, slightly rough. Very masculine. She returned the kiss, seeking him as he sought her, relishing the hardness of him, in the beauty of sensation that made her feel both faint and very, very alive. Sparks touched her system, trembling throughout her, seizing her, releasing her. He created a hunger in her, something so strong it couldn't be denied. She wanted to forget the world around them and know more of him. She wanted to have him beside her, holding her, naked, touching her. . . .

He raised his head, smiling as he stared down at her dazed eyes. He steadied her. "Tomorrow, Donna," he murmured, and then he was gone.

Donna watched his dark-clad back and broad shoulders as he walked down the hallway. She echoed a small sound of horror and shame and slammed the door, closing her eyes as she leaned heavily against it.

She groaned aloud, shaking. A priest! Dear Lord, a priest had kissed her, and she had wanted it. Wanted much, much more. She had wanted to lie beside him, to make love to him. She! A woman who had spent twelve years in Catholic schools. Oh, if the nuns could see her now. Donna Miro, falling for—a priest.

"No . . . no . . . no!" she whispered in dismay. Her face flamed a brilliant red and she raced the few feet to the bed, throwing herself on it to rock back and forth. What was happening to her, and what in heaven and hell was going on?

CHAPTER SIX

Luke entered his bedroom and stripped off his jacket with un-customary speed, tugging at a sleeve while combing through his closet. He saw what he wanted—a pea-green, tattered army sweater. A moment later he was tugging on the sweater and replacing his dress pants with a pair of worn jeans. He started out his bedroom door, but a slight sound alerted him to turn back.

A figure, shrouded by the darkness, was crawling through the garden window. It straightened and stared at Luke.

Both men were of equal height. The intruder was slimmer, and the character of his face was masked by a dense growth of beard and an untrimmed mustache. The dark hair on his head was as wild and tangled as his beard; his clothing more tattered than Luke's old army-issue sweater.

But Luke smiled at his sorry-looking visitor and quietly closed his bedroom door. He drew the drapes before flicking on a light, then embraced the shaggy man briefly before indicating the plush period chair that sat before the garden window.

"Have a seat, Andrew," he encouraged. "I was just about to come looking for you."

Andrew leaned back in the chair and closed his eyes wearily for a minute. He rubbed his temple with his thumb and forefingers. "I figured you would, that's why I tried to beat you to it. No sense the two of us crawling around different ghettos trying to find one another." He opened his eyes at last. "You got anything decent to drink around here?"

Luke chuckled softly and strode to a small carved cabinet. He pulled out a bottle of Jack Daniels and offered it to Andrew. Andrew smiled like a high-school kid as he took the bottle, twisted off the top, and drank a long gulp. He straightened the bottle, shuddered slightly, and returned it to Luke.

"Damn—sorry, Father, but that was good. After all that rot gut I've been drinking with the winos!"

"Bad day?" Luke queried.

"Yeah—even before I heard from Tricia." He gazed at Luke accusingly. "How on earth did you stumble into Donna Miro—and why did you tell her that you knew me?"

Luke shrugged and decided to take a swig of the Jack Daniels himself. "That was exactly it—I stumbled into her. She was trying to find an address from a letter *you* wrote her and was in the process of being mugged when I found her."

"Oh," Andrew murmured. "Have you got a cigarette, Luke?"

Luke patiently obliged him.

Andrew inhaled deeply, then grimaced. "Much, much better than the butts I've been smoking all day!"

Luke tensed. "How long do you think this is going to go on?"

Andrew lifted his brows and shrugged helplessly. "I wish I knew. Hey—you're supposedly the one with the pipeline to the Almighty. Can't you pray any harder that we nab this guy?"

He had tried to be flippant and easy, and he knew that his effort had failed miserably when he watched Luke tense, pain filling his eyes before he turned away.

Andrew watched, his hands clenched together tightly behind his back. "Hey, Luke, I'm sorry. I know if anyone has been praying—"

Luke turned back to him, then sat at the foot of the bed, raking his fingers through his hair. "I don't know. Sometimes I think I'm better off not to feel so viciously that he must be caught. I'm a priest, Drew. I shouldn't hate this guy so much."

"You're a human being. You wouldn't be normal if you didn't hate him after . . . what happened."

Luke said nothing for a minute, lighting a cigarette himself. He watched a mist of smoke fade away. "Have you been able to see Mom lately?"

"Last week." He grimaced, then smiled ruefully again, feeling that the tension was past. "I sometimes hate to go see her. She spends the whole time moaning over my hair."

Luke laughed so hard he choked. "Hey, she's your mother. What do you want?"

"Ah, Mom's a good old girl, I guess. She worries about us both, you know."

"Yeah, I know. But I'm okay."

"I know you are."

The brothers gazed at one another for a minute, then both smiled.

"So, tell me, what's she like?"

"Donna Miro?"

"Yeah."

"She's . . ."

"Gorgeous," Andrew supplied. Luke arched a curious brow. "I was watching you two when you entered the hotel."

"You do manage to get around this city—and be in the right place at the right time," Luke murmured.

"Did you tell her that we're related?"

"I didn't tell her anything, and certainly nothing that might imperil your cover. I just figured that if anyone could get you, it would be Trish. And then it would be up to you. You do know about her, don't you?"

"Yeah," Andrew said dryly. "Lorna has mentioned her to me several times. Or, I should say, when she's talking to me at all, she talks about Donna and her family." He hesitated. "When we first met, she told me a lot about the Miros. Lorna's an only child of older parents who died when she was in college. But from what I understand, she used to spend all her time with them even when she was a kid."

Luke emitted a sigh of exasperation. "Then you must have expected someone to come around looking for Lorna! If she is close to this girl—"

"She promised me that she'd taken care of it!" Andrew exclaimed with annoyance. "The little"—he glanced at his brother and apparently amended his thought—"witch!"

Luke chuckled softly. "She was once the most beautiful woman you had ever seen. What happened?"

"How do I know? She's impossible!"

"She's probably frightened—and she has every right to be."

"She should have a little more faith in me." He sighed. "It

61

really doesn't matter. I haven't seen her in a while—and it will probably be awhile before I can see her again."

Luke shrugged, but his eyes twinkled a warm gold in the artificial light. "Things will improve eventually."

"Umm. Someday this will end, and Lorna can go home and be entirely out of my hair."

"I see. Can't wait to get her completely out of sight—and mind?"

"Definitely."

Luke had no reply, so he turned away before his brother could see his laughter. Andrew had always been high on freedom. Adventuresome, independent. It was difficult for him to accept the fact that he was falling in love with his key witness. So difficult that he was refusing to accept it.

"Well, what are you going to do about Donna Miro?"

"I don't know," Andrew murmured. "But it's sure given me one hell of a headache. Damn that Lorna! She should have said she was taking an Alaskan cruise or something."

"Well, yes, I'd say something should have been done differently. You're going to have to come up with something now. The truth would probably be the best bet. Donna Miro is determined. She isn't going to give up."

"My superiors will play havoc with this one." Andrew moaned.

"It isn't your fault."

"Yes, it is. Lorna is my responsibility."

"I wouldn't worry. It will work out."

"I hope so. I've been at this so long. And. . . ." He paused, glancing at his brother again. "I hope so," he repeated.

Luke sighed. "You don't have to tiptoe with my feelings, Andrew. It's been a long time now."

"It must still hurt."

"It does. It always will. But it's more important that we solve everything now. No matter how hard I prayed, I couldn't change the past. But I do believe in the future."

"God's will?" Andrew asked his brother dryly.

Luke gave him a half smile. "I guess you've got me there, Drew. Yeah, God's will. It will work out."

Andrew began to drum his fingers on the arm of the chair. "I guess I'll have to tell her the truth, or else I could wind up in trouble."

"Yeah, that's why I think you should make sure you arrive here looking half respectable tomorrow night."

"Well, if I tell her the truth, she can check out my story."

"And put herself into possible danger if she's seen by the wrong people."

"Damn Lorna! This thing is so fragile!"

"That's true. And you've put a hell of a lot into being Andrew 'McKennon'—bum, wino, et cetera. You've put months and months of your life into it. Almost a year. . . ." Luke paused suddenly; he couldn't help it. It hurt to remember when it had all begun—because it had all begun with April's death. And when he thought about April, he still felt a sense of shock settling over him. It couldn't be . . . and yet it was. Shock became that horrible sense of loss and pain—and helpless fury at that loss. He had to remind himself that he was a priest with a strong belief. April did not lie in the ground; she had entered a higher place. Life was something that he had learned to live without her—with the aid of his faith. If he could help, it had to be the *living* whom he helped. But no matter what his faith, he was human. He wanted the murderer caught. He wanted his brother to lead a saner life. And, God help him, more than anything, he wanted Lorna Doria to live and come out of everything okay.

Luke drew in a deep breath and continued. "This has cost you a great deal of personal happiness. It's cost everyone . . . so much. Donna is a problem, but I think if it's explained to her properly, she'll accept it all and just lay low. The truth will be the best bet, Andrew. I don't think she'd accept anything but. And if she nosed around elsewhere, you could be out of a good cover. The newspapers would hop all over the story."

"Yeah," Andrew said thoughtfully. "I guess I'd better make the best possible impression." He paused for a minute, then gazed at his brother again. "They want to see you down at headquarters again."

A pained expression passed quickly over Luke's handsome features. "I've tried, Drew. You know that. I just come up with a blank wall."

"Different case—and I don't need help on the other one. I

know what's going on. I just have to figure out how to prove it."
Andrew shook his head, as if to clear it from the problem that
had long plagued his days and nights. "They need help bad on
what they suspect to be a kidnapping. No clues except a scrap
of cloth."

"Tell them I'll be in on Monday," Luke said.

"They'll appreciate it."

"Yeah. I think they're afraid of me."

"No." Andrew laughed. "Not you, Luke. They're a bit in
awe of you. You're a priest, and I guess they really think you
have a direct line to heavenly assistance."

"Great," Luke muttered.

"Hey, what difference does it make? You can help sometimes,
and you know it."

"I'll be there."

Andrew stood regretfully, looking back at the comfortable,
well-padded Victorian chair. "I guess I'll go haunt St. Patricks,
then head downtown. Got another cigarette?"

"Take the pack."

Andrew accepted it, grinning. "Poor Mom and Dad! They
were hoping for a lawyer and a doctor and they got an over-
grown hippie and a crazy guru."

"Speak for yourself!" Luke laughed. "My bishops would be
horrified by your description of one of their priests!"

Andrew chuckled again, then slipped silently out the window, the same way he had come. Luke stared after his brother a
long while, then thoughtfully stripped down to the buff and
crawled into bed.

He didn't sleep. He stared out the window to the garden
beyond and watched the way the moonbeams created shadow
and light. He hadn't felt quite so restless in a long time.

It was the girl, of course. He hadn't felt quite so affected by a
woman in a long, long time. Maybe never. When he was near
her, all he wanted to do was reach out and touch her. He smiled
in the darkness, fully aware that she felt the same tension drawing them together and that it horrified her.

He rolled over suddenly, wondering why he had decided to
trust her when it threw a new problem right in his brother's lap.
No, he'd had little choice. She might have gone elsewhere. And

she might have wound up in all the wrong places at all the wrong time.

It was strange. He had just met her, but she had already eased him somewhat. For the first time in months, he hadn't thought about April, not until Andrew's arrival. That was the way of things, he told himself wryly. Life went on for the living. Human nature. A time to mourn, a time to live again. A new love—not to replace the lost, but to exist strong and sure on its own.

Luke laughed aloud and twisted around to lie comfortably on his pillow. Love! He'd just met her. But he was attracted. So attracted, he was almost afraid of being close. She'd really be shocked if a priest swept her into his arms, tossed her onto her bed, and made desperate, passionate love to her!

But, oh, what a lovely dream!

St. Philip's Episcopal Church.
Episcopal!

Oh, what an idiot she had been! She should have known—she should have realized the truth about "Father Luke." She had just been conditioned all her life to believe that a man called priest was naturally a Roman Catholic.

He wasn't. He was Protestant. Episcopalian. Donna closed her eyes for a minute, angry but smiling dryly. To her grandfather, anyone who wasn't a Roman Catholic was a bit of a heathen.

Donna repeated the simple fact in her mind. Luke Trudeau wasn't a Roman Catholic. He wasn't sworn to a celibate life.

Great. She had spent her night wondering if there really was a hell where she might burn in torment forever for lusting after a priest and he was an Episcopalian, allowed by his religion to marry, to love a woman. And he had known that she thought him a Roman Catholic and he had played on her sense of morality with a great deal of amusement. Damn him! Even if he was a priest!

"Donna? We should really go in. The service is about to begin."

Donna mechanically curled her lips into a smile for Tricia. "Yes, heaven forbid! I'd hate to walk in late and disturb the service."

Tricia, who had arrived at the Plaza at precisely four with a waiting taxi, looked confused by her tone of voice. Donna tried to make her smile into something more sincere. She failed miserably; she was too angry to smile. But she slipped an arm through the other woman's and led the way down the walk to the church.

"It's beautiful," she murmured inanely, needing something to say.

"Yes, isn't it? It's one of the oldest churches in Manhattan. The stained glass was brought from England, and a lot of the marble came from Italy. It really is a beautiful church."

Donna smiled her reply because they had entered the small apse. There was a peaceful quiet within the church—one that almost negated her feeling of anger, but didn't quite succeed. She still felt as if she had been taken for a fool as she followed Tricia into a back pew and knelt beside her, lowering her head in silent prayer. Nothing came to mind except for the itching desire to slap a too-handsome priest across the face.

The chorus began to sing, accompanied by the strains of an organ, several flutes, and a number of softly strummed guitars. She saw Luke then, as the service began. His voice was deep and husky, pleasantly resonant as it carried throughout the church. She didn't hear the service, just his voice.

He wore black and white robes, and despite her anger, Donna found herself dropping her eyes. Even if he was an Episcopalian, she was somewhat ashamed of her thoughts. They were extremely irreligious. She didn't hear the words of prayer, just the rise and fall of his husky tenor, and it seemed that her stomach formed knots as she listened.

And then, to her dismay, she discovered that his eyes had locked with hers. The fire within them seemed to ignite a burning low within her belly. Eternity passed—or was it just moments? She looked about herself. Nothing was amiss. But it was, it was. She was sitting through a church service, and all she could think about was this man.

But it was all right to think about him. Episcopalian priests married, but did they become involved in affairs? An affair? The last thing she would want from him would be an affair. Then what did she want? Marriage? Oh, what was she thinking about? She still wanted to kill him.

She looked at her hands and discovered that her fingers were trembling, as if they too were lost in memory of touching the dark hair that curled over his collar, feeling the hard knot of muscle in his shoulders as they danced.

Donna took a deep breath. She hadn't even been thinking about Lorna or about her coming interview with Andrew McKennon, the man she was there this evening to see.

Tricia gave her a nudge on the arm, and Donna glanced up, startled. "The collection plate!" Tricia prodded her. Donna turned guiltily to the woman on her left and accepted the silver dish. She fumbled for two dollar bills to slip into it, then passed it on to Tricia, who smiled at her peculiarly.

Donna took a deep breath, finding that she could finally pray. She prayed for the service to end.

The chorus began to sing again, and Tricia was leading her out of the church. "We might as well walk around to the rectory," Tricia said. "Luke will be busy for a while yet, but I'm willing to bet that Mary will have coffee and tea and some pastry ready."

Donna nodded. She felt a little foolish suddenly, as if her mind and imagination had carried her away. When she wasn't near Luke, when she didn't see him or hear him, she could convince herself that she was being absurd.

Lorna—and Andrew McKennon. She had to remember her priorities. Very soon, hopefully, she would discover that her "faith" had been well founded and that Lorna was fine. And then she could go home, leave New York, and forget the Reverend Lucien Trudeau.

Did she really want to leave? And could she leave? There could be no simple answer to all the mystery surrounding Lorna's disappearance.

Nor could there be a simple answer to the mystery of Luke Trudeau. He was no ordinary priest, and he was no ordinary man. Nor was the feeling that engulfed her when she was near him.

Andrew McKennon could solve at least one of her mysteries. And she was due to see him very soon.

Donna glanced at Tricia as they began to walk, remembering that she had promised to go by faith and not ask questions. But it had seemed last night that Tricia was not so alarmed at being questioned and that Donna just might get a few answers.

"Tricia," she murmured suddenly, "how well do you know Lorna?"

"Oh, fairly well." Tricia smiled. "Well enough to like her very much."

"I'm glad," Donna murmured.

"So am I." Tricia laughed.

"And . . . and Andrew McKennon?"

Tricia smiled again. "I've known Andrew for years. He's as close as a brother. And so is Luke."

Donna tried hard to conceal a grimace. She couldn't think of the "Father" as anyone's brother. His attitude toward the fairer sex just didn't seem to be very fraternal or paternal.

"Luke is a wonderful man," Tricia said.

"Oh, yes, dandy," Donna returned.

Tricia suddenly stopped walking. It was growing dark around them, but the street was tree-lined and surrounded by rare, propertied residential homes. A few blocks away there might be slums, but this was an upper-class Manhattan neighborhood.

The congregation at St. Philip's was apparently a varied one, some very rich, and some very poor.

"Luke has asked me not to tell you too much, Donna, and I have to respect those wishes because there is a very good reason for them. But I want to assure you the best that I can. Everything possible is being done to keep Lorna safe."

"To *keep* her safe?" Donna pressed, feeling a little guilty. Tricia was going to go out on a limb to confide in her, and she wasn't sure that she deserved such consideration.

"I—I can't say any more."

Donna felt as if her heart was hammering inside her chest. "I won't repeat anything that you tell me," she said, and she knew, from the trust and sincerity in Tricia's eyes, that she would be bound to keep that promise.

"Lorna is in protective custody."

Donna's breath seemed to constrict in her throat. Protective custody? How did Tricia mean it? Had Lorna done something? She couldn't believe it. No, no, the key word was "protective." Lorna had seen something or heard something, protective custody. Whose custody? The police had denied knowing anything.

68

"What do you mean, Tricia? Why didn't Luke tell me that?" she asked.

"Luke wouldn't have told you anything he felt he shouldn't —and I can't explain further because you shouldn't know anything right now. You shouldn't even be seeing Andrew now. I'm surprised that Luke called me, and I'm even more surprised that Andrew agreed to see you."

"But why . . . ?"

"Donna, one day, hopefully soon, you can be told everything. But not now and not from me! Please? Andrew may explain the whole thing tonight. Can you let it go at that?"

"I can try," Donna promised. Blind faith, she thought. She would try.

Tricia smiled vaguely and they continued walking on to the rectory. Their conversation was idle. Donna really was trying to keep her word, even though anxiety and curiosity seemed to be consuming her alive.

She learned that Tricia had always lived in New York and loved it; Tricia was amused by Donna's tales about her despotic grandfather and lovable mother.

"She really irons underwear?" Tricia chuckled incredulously.

"Yes. My brothers always had the neatest-looking jockeys in the locker room."

They were both smiling as they walked up the path to the house that Donna had been carried along the night before. Mary was apparently expecting them. She threw open the door and greeted them warmly. "Girls, there's coffee, tea, and cakes on the cart in the study. Luke suggested I make myself scarce for the evening so I'm doing just that."

Donna started to protest, but Mary was already grabbing her hat and coat. "I'm going to meet my sister just down the street, so don't fret on my account!"

She left the two of them. Tricia—apparently very comfortable in her surroundings—led the way back into the study. Donna remembered the room all too well herself.

Tricia poured herself a cup of coffee and took one of the little scones sitting on the tray. "Luke should be along any minute now. Andrew . . . well, he should be right along too."

Donna poured her own coffee and wandered around the room. She had a probing question she wanted to ask, and if she was going to ask it, she knew she had better get it out before Luke appeared. "Tricia," she asked, trying to sound casual, "was April Luke's wife?"

Tricia seemed surprised that she knew about April at all. "Why, yes, yes, she was."

"She's . . . dead?"

Tricia hesitated, only the fraction of a second. "Yes, she died about a year ago."

"What happened?"

Again Tricia hesitated. And this time, before she could speak, the door to the study suddenly burst open, and Luke was standing there.

He had changed. He wore jeans and a short-sleeved, open-necked Wrangler shirt. His eyes were focused on Tricia as if he knew she had been divulging secrets.

"Good evening, ladies," he murmured, still staring pointedly at Tricia. "I'm not interrupting anything, am I?"

CHAPTER SEVEN

"Not at all, not at all, Luke!" Tricia murmured. She flushed uneasily. "Well, now that you're here, I guess I'd better get going. I've an early morning tomorrow. Mondays, you know."

"Don't go, Tricia!" Donna heard herself exclaim. Why did she feel as if she needed someone in the room to act as a buffer between them? Easy. She wanted to strangle him—and she wanted to hold him, touch him. Stay, Tricia, stay, she begged silently.

"Oh, but I really have to," Tricia murmured. She smiled and impulsively kissed Donna's cheek. "I hope I get to see you again before you leave New York." She hurried away, smiling uneasily as she came to Luke in the doorway. "Good night, Luke," she said, standing on tiptoe to kiss his cheek.

A smile of subtle amusement filled out the taut line that had been his mouth. "You really don't have to go, Tricia."

"But I think I will," she told him.

Donna felt a little stab of jealousy at the look that passed between them. He might have been angry with her, but there was an understanding and affection that crossed between them that somehow touched Donna deeply.

That same little knot that had twisted in her stomach at the church was with her again. Her knees felt wobbly, and worse, she felt a shaky heat. She still didn't like the look in his verdant green and gold eyes when they fell on her; it was an alert and wary look, as if he trusted her as far as he could throw a bag of bricks. It was his "dangerous" look, as she was coming to think of it; she could not forget that whatever his denomination, he was not your usual, peace-loving priest. But there was more to that look than anger or guarded wariness. She still felt assessed, as if his eyes caressed her, knew her. Golden hunger gleamed within them—and that ever-present amusement.

And Donna still wasn't sure if she wanted to slap him for making a fool of her, or run into his arms and beg that he touch her again.

Tricia slipped from the room unnoticed. Luke entered it and closed the door behind him.

"Did you enjoy the service?" he asked her politely.

"Tremendously," she murmured dryly. "It was extremely similar to a *Roman* Catholic service." She wanted to lash into him with utter fury; she wanted to stay as cool and calm as he was. She could feel her own tension, like static all about her, yet she was going to try—try!—to hear what avenue of explanation he would take now.

"Yes, well," Luke said casually, "the services would be similar. The denominations are extremely close."

He was still baiting her. Donna smiled. "Yes, well, I do know a little about it. The Episcopalian Church is the Church of England—formed because Henry the Eighth wanted a divorce, isn't that the story?" Her tone was sardonic, and it irked her that she was stooping to attack his religion because she just felt that she had to.

But he seemed undaunted by her opinion and unaware of her sarcasm.

"Well, yes and no," Luke answered easily enough, pouring himself a cup of coffee. "The trouble actually began long before that. Henry the Second was against the power of the church—and it coincided with the power of the state. He had a right to be annoyed, actually. Anyone claiming to be a 'cleric' could claim refuge from the law. And one in every fifty people could read the few prayers that classified one as a cleric."

"Ah, so the church was corrupt!" Donna said dryly.

Luke lowered his eyes, but a small smile played about his lips. "No, the church was not corrupt. Men were corrupt."

Donna turned away. She would be an absolute fool to argue theology with a priest!

"At least you really are a priest," she muttered.

"Did you doubt that?"

"Sometimes."

"Really?" He truthfully seemed surprised.

72

"Maybe not completely, but I've certainly never met another priest quite like you."

"Meaning?"

"I don't know exactly . . ." Donna began to murmur. Then she gave up pretending that she was staring into the darkness beyond the garden window. She swung about to face him. The hell with remaining calm and cool. She was furious, and she had a right to be. "You're the first lascivious priest I've ever met!"

He laughed, and the sound was deep and husky, sending those little currents he could create racing along her spine. Dear God, it was terrible. The man could recite a litany, and just hearing that caress of his voice could knot her stomach into a pit of heat.

"Ah, Ms. Miro! Must I repeat myself? I am a priest, but not a saint."

"Not a god, just a man?" Donna taunted.

"Very much a man, I'm afraid, Donna."

Too much a man, she decided as he started walking toward her, still smiling. And as he walked toward her, he looked more like a rugged cowboy from a Marlboro ad than a priest should ever have a right to look. His face seemed very tanned against the light blue of the shirt, his neck appeared long and strong, and at the open V of his collar, she could see the beginning of little fluffs of dark hair that surely covered his chest. The muscles in his arms seemed to strain against the short, rolled sleeves of his shirt.

She thought how much she would like to see him take that shirt off, how much she would like to be crushed against his chest, feeling the splay of his fingers in her hair again, the touch of his lips that both demanded and cajoled . . .

She interrupted her own fantasy with inner fury. He had let her suffer through a night of miserable torment, and he had damned well known it! He was playing some game of secrecy over something she was determined to expose, and for all she knew, he might be engaged in some kind of criminal activity.

"Donna . . ." He began as he came close to her.

"Don't come near me!" she snapped furiously. "You—oh, I don't even know what to call you! You knew all the while that I came from an extremely Catholic home and you led me on to

73

believe . . . how could you? And you had the bloody damn nerve to find it all amusing—"

"Donna!" He interrupted her, and she knew that her rising temper had set a flame to his. He was quiet and controlled but no longer calm or unruffled. "I just let you go by your own self-righteous assumptions."

"Self-righteous assumptions!" she exclaimed, gasping in a deep breath. "My assumptions weren't self-righteous—they were natural. And you know it! You know exactly what I thought, and how I would feel, and then last night, at the door —oh, I know precisely how to say it! You are a scurvy, low-blooded heel!"

"Donna!" He said, and it seemed that he was torn by the same emotions, anger and need. His voice gentled slightly. "Perhaps I did play you along, but only because it was so obvious. And I'm not really a lascivious man—"

"Oh, no? You seem very well versed in what you're doing. Do they teach kissing at the seminaries these days? The art of se-duction?"

"Of course not," he snapped angrily.

"Then—"

"Men aren't born priests, and there is a very major difference between Roman Catholic and Episcopalian—or Protestant—clergymen."

"I know," Donna breathed. Yes, she knew he had been mar-ried, and he had probably been running around long before that marriage. He knew his effect, he knew exactly what he was doing. He had that streak of assurance. Was he so worldly, and she so innocent? Suddenly she was very afraid of him, and an-grier still.

He reached out to touch her. She had pitched her temper into such a blaze of fury that she was wild. She instinctively raised a hand to strike him, but discovered that she was entirely impo-tent because she was in his arms, crushed hard against the wall of his chest.

"Stop it!" he snapped, and a fire, a blaze of fury seemed to burn deeply in his eyes.

"No," she murmured, but all she could do was pound limply against his back, mumble a protest against his chest. "Don't!

74

Please, let me go, this isn't right, I don't understand you, I don't trust you, and I don't—"

She stopped speaking on a thin breath of fading air. The fire in his eyes had become a field of warm, beckoning embers. His hold about her lost the tension of anger; it remained firm but gentled, and she felt a tenderness in the arms that refused to let her go.

"Donna," he murmured. "Don't you see? It's . . . you."

His voice reached out to her, embraced and caressed her. There was confusion in it, as if he were a little awed; pained, as if he would rather he didn't feel the magic, but refused to deny it.

"I-I don't . . . Luke. . . ."

Her words died away as she felt her head tilted back and his mouth claiming hers, moving slowly, provocatively. Making her forget, again, that anything else mattered. His heart—she could feel it again. And the heat of him. A wonderful, powerful heat, encompassing her, draining her, giving her strength. She couldn't have broken away from him had she wanted to. From the moment she had seen him, she had known he was different. A man to make his own rules, to know what he wanted, to go straight for it.

He wanted her, and she was shamefully easy for the taking. He could gaze at her and make her long for his touch. And when he touched her, when his lips moved over hers, knowing them, exploring them, kissing her until she was breathless, holding her close, moving his hands along her shoulders and back, her spine, her hips. . . .

"Donna," he murmured again, his lips still against hers, his breath a husky whisper of air. He kissed the corners of her lips, rimmed the tip of his tongue around them, tasting, adoring. He kissed her forehead, and her eyelids, and then he found her mouth again, ravaging it with his tongue, sending sparks of fire to spiral with the knot of longing in the pit of her belly. She couldn't speak, she could only lean against him and pray that it could go on and on. . . .

She heard a sound, but she was so lost in the tempest of growing desire that at first it meant nothing to her. She was dizzy and breathless, barely aware that there was a real world. She knew the feel of the man who held her, the taste of his lips, the heat and strength of his arms, the scent that compelled and excited and encompassed her. Nothing else.

The sound came again. She was released, and Donna stared up at Luke with confusion. Then she realized what the sound had been. A warning. An intruder, politely clearing his throat. . . .

There was another man in the room. The door was closed, but it was possible that it had opened and she hadn't heard it. Someone might have even pounded on it and she might not have heard it.

Her teeth were suddenly chattering; she felt a chill. Had he come through the window? But why? And how much had he witnessed?

She struggled to gather her thoughts. Andrew McKennon! She had come here to meet Andrew McKennon. But why had he come through the window? Why?

Dear Lord, nothing was making sense, much less her sudden passion for a man she barely knew. And now, here at last was Andrew McKennon. The man who had the answers. She had wanted him to realize that she was persistent and dignified—determined and tenacious. But instead he had found her entangled in a very passionate kiss. It was not quite the way she wanted to impress a man when she was going to demand answers from him.

"Good evening," Andrew said. Beneath a shaggy beard, he had a smile of secret amusement very much like Luke's. But it was a surprisingly nice smile, just as his eyes were a surprisingly warm green. And his voice was pleasant, his words soft-spoken.

Luke's scowl had the appearance of a dangerously brooding thundercloud. "Damn it, Andrew. I'm accustomed to you coming through my window, and normally I don't mind. But I wish you'd learn to knock on the wall or something."

"I tried to clear my throat! No one was paying attention."

"How hard did you try?"

"I am sorry to interrupt, Luke." The newcomer chuckled.

"I'm sure you are," Luke replied dryly, his anger apparently controlled and perhaps fading. After all, Andrew McKennon was *the* guest of the evening.

They were both nuts. Completely off the wall, Donna decided. And she had to be just as crazy to be standing here, listening to this absurd exchange. Andrew McKennon always came through the window?

McKennon turned to Donna, still smiling. "Personally, Miss Miro, I think he deserved a slap much more than a kiss."

She was too dumbfounded to speak. Shamed, embarrassed, horrified—and more confused than ever. Luke hadn't completely released her, but that was probably for the best, because she was still shaking ridiculously.

The man who had appeared as mysteriously as a genie from a magic lamp stepped forward, grinning with a wicked appeal that rivaled Luke's. Donna noted that despite the unkempt appearance of his hair and beard, he smelled clean, and that his worn jeans and denim shirt were laundered and fresh. He seemed about the same age as Luke, perhaps a year or two either way.

He stretched out an arm, offering a hand to her. "You're Donna. I'm Andrew McKennon. I'm sorry I've been so difficult to find, but I'm afraid it's all been necessary."

She stared at the hand outstretched to her. She felt Luke's arm about her waist, encouraging her forward.

A little stream of tremors rippled along her back and settled in her spine. She had come to New York believing the worst of this man. She had been certain that he had preyed on Lorna, that he had somehow hurt her, or taken her in a con game.

But now the stakes seemed far higher than a mere con game. If she could believe Tricia, Lorna was being held for her own safety. So what did that make this stranger with the shaggy appearance?

Donna searched his eyes quickly. Quick, alert, knowing. Very green, and very sharp. As if they had seen a lot.

Donna sighed. She had met a strange priest, and in twenty-four hours everything had changed. She didn't understand who she was herself anymore so how could she really understand who Andrew McKennon was?

But everything was still wrong. There were no answers. She was being told to trust the situation on faith, but why was she meeting him at night, and why was everything about Andrew McKennon such a dark secret?

"Donna?" He said her name lightly, but there seemed to be a tense appeal that hung in the air.

If she took his hand, she accepted him. She accepted the mystery. She put her faith blindly in a priest who had drawn her into a tempest of emotion and passion.

Donna still hesitated. She knew somehow that she would enter a misted maze and that she would not know if she would ever find her way through.

"Donna?" Luke spoke even more lightly than Andrew. Apparently his anger at the interruption had entirely faded. It seemed that the two men knew one another very well. Teasing was one thing, business was another.

And this meeting was important somehow to both men. Luke's voice did not carry appeal; it carried the demand: Trust him, trust me; I have trusted you.

She couldn't ignore that voice. God help her, she didn't know why, but she couldn't. She stretched out her own hand to accept the one offered to her.

She had to clear her throat. "Hello, Andrew. I-I've been trying to meet you for some time."

CHAPTER EIGHT

"I guess the first thing that I have to do," Andrew told her, "is ask that you keep everything you are about to hear entirely confidential."

Donna glanced at him and then at Luke, warily.

"I know I'm asking a lot," Andrew said softly.

"I really have no reason to trust you," Donna said. She felt Luke squeeze her arm. "But I guess I'm going to."

Andrew moved into the room, helping himself to a cup of coffee. "Why don't you sit down, Donna? This could be a long explanation."

Donna moved to the couch and sat. Andrew was in one corner of the room, Luke in the other. She felt as if she had been placed between a pair of uncaged Bengal tigers. And they wanted trust?

"About a year ago," Andrew began, "New York City became plagued by a strange string of robberies."

"The 'church robberies' you and Tricia were talking about yesterday?" Donna asked Luke. Luke nodded but remained silent. Donna glanced at Andrew. He seemed to be waiting for Luke to speak, but when Luke didn't, he began his explanation again.

"The robber, mugger—or whatever you want to call him—started attacking single women coming and going from church. Obvious motive crimes, or so it would appear. The method of attack was always the same—one man, catching the woman alone. We're not sure yet, though, if it's always the same man. In which case, these robberies are planned. The man always wears a dark stocking over his head, and not one victim has ever been able to identify her attacker. They've been armed robberies, but no one was ever shot. The mugger strikes his victims over the head. One of the"—Andrew paused for a brief moment, then continued—"one of the first victims later died from head injuries. So suddenly we were after more than a petty robber—we were after a murderer."

Donna swallowed suddenly, unnerved and also sure that she had missed something important. "I don't understand where you fit into this, Mr. McKennon. Or what it has to do with Lorna."

Andrew flashed her a brief, grim smile. "I'm getting to that, Donna. First of all, my name isn't really McKennon. It's Trudeau."

Donna gasped and stared at Luke with angry accusation.

He shrugged, still refusing to speak and apparently undaunted by his deceit.

"Then you two are brothers," she stated sharply.

"Yes."

"I really don't understand—"

"I'm a detective with N.Y.P.D. I've been working undercover on this case for almost a year. I've been living on the streets and eating in the soup kitchens, trying to get some kind of word from the street grapevine."

"Oh . . . but I've been to the police! Why did they deny everything?"

Andrew sighed, taking a seat beside her, clasping and unclasping his hands in an idle gesture. Luke finally stepped up and began to talk, settling at her side on one knee and taking the fingers of her left hand into his own.

"Donna, while he was working on the streets, Andrew learned that the crimes were not as obvious as it appeared. The 'robber' or 'robbers'—whichever the case may be—were hired to rob and paid a much higher sum than the money and jewelry stolen."

Donna was truly confused and truly frightened. "I don't understand."

Luke straightened and idly paced before the low coffee table. "Someone was planning the 'perfect' crime."

"Donna," Andrew said, stepping back into the conversation, "nine out of ten times when a murder is committed, the police look first to the family. The wife, the child, and so on. And we're not quite as bumbling as some people would like to make us out to be. We do catch most of those types of murderers."

"Crimes of passion are often very easy," Luke said. "Crimes with financial motive can be even easier."

"Now I'm really confused," Donna murmured.

"It is confusing and that's why we've got all this subterfuge going on," Andrew said.

"At the end of August," Luke told her, "another of the mugger's victims died. Her name was Hattie Simson. She was a very wealthy woman, and the majority stockholder in a company called Lithtin."

"Her grandson," Andrew continued, "was naturally distraught by her death. Too distraught. We discovered that he had been trying to wrest the old lady's power from her for a long, long time."

Donna felt a headache coming on; her mind was whirling, but she felt she was at last beginning to understand.

"I—I think I understand. This man wanted to kill his grandmother, so he staged a number of armed robberies so that when she was killed, suspicion would never fall on him, because it would appear that she was killed by someone the police were already stalking?"

"Exactly."

"Oh, God," Donna whispered, feeling ill. "But what . . . what does Lorna have to do with this?"

"Lorna stumbled onto the crime," Luke said. "She happened to be in the wrong place at the wrong time. She saw the man who struck Mrs. Simson, and she saw another man, the driver of the car that the killer ran to in order to make his escape."

"And she can identify them both?"

"Yes."

"Then why don't you arrest them?"

Andrew glanced at Luke, then sighed. "It's not that simple. A good defense attorney could rip her apart on a witness stand. The night was dark, et cetera, et cetera. And I haven't been able to find the man who actually committed the robbery and murder."

"Donna, newspaper reporters tried to interview Lorna right after the crime. There were policemen all over the place, but suddenly shots started ringing out from a nearby building. She was grazed across the shoulder, and that's why she went into the hospital."

"She was hurt!" Donna cried out in horror.

"Not badly, only a flesh wound," Luke assured her. "But there was no record of her having been at the hospital because the police knew then that someone would rather have Lorna dead than able to talk to anyone about what she had seen."

"So where is she now?" Donna asked.

Both men were silent.

"Where is she?" Donna persisted angrily.

"I don't want to tell you where she is, Miss Miro," Andrew said softly. "You would be tempted to try to get there, to see her, write to her, or call her."

"But why can't I?"

"Donna," Luke said, "we believe that Hal Simson killed his grandmother—or paid an assassin to kill her—for control of the company. At her death he became an extremely wealthy man. We've always suspected that he had links with the underworld. He has a network system of information that would put A.T. and T. to shame. He can hire dozens of paid assassins. The only way we could possibly keep Lorna safe was to make her disappear absolutely—so that no one could find her."

"You can't even trust me?" Donna whispered.

"Donna," Luke murmured, "it isn't a matter of trusting you. We don't want you getting involved, and we don't want you leading anyone to Lorna."

Andrew laughed. "I have to stay so low myself that I crawl through windows to see my own brother. Can you understand what a horribly tenuous position we're in?"

"Yes," Donna said, feeling numb, "I—I guess I can." She glanced sharply at Andrew. "What has Tricia to do with this?"

"She's my partner, Donna. The club where she works is very elite, but it also hosts a number of our shadier businessmen. She's hoping to pick up something there."

Donna glanced at Luke. "Luke," she murmured, "I want you to swear to me that this is all true. Word for word true."

"It's true, Donna. I swear it."

"So . . ." She took a deep breath and stared at Andrew. "What do I do?"

"Go home, Donna. Trust me, and trust the N.Ÿ.P.D."

"How can I just go home?" Donna asked miserably. "I'll be worried day and night."

"I'm working as hard as I can to come up with enough evidence to arrest Simson," Andrew assured her. "I swear to you that Lorna is well and safe. Please, trust us. If something leaked to the papers now, the whole case could be blown before it really gets started. And if anything at all were to give away Lorna's whereabouts . . . well, it could be fatal."

"Oh, God!" Donna groaned.

"Donna," Luke said softly. "Andrew just assured you that Lorna is well and fine." He glanced at his brother. "And actually," he added more lightly, "it's not as grim as you think. Lorna is determined to see this man arrested, and she actually considers it all to be an extremely important adventure."

"Yeah, she considers it an adventure," Andrew said dryly.

There were undercurrents there, Donna decided, that she didn't quite understand. She instinctively trusted Andrew, just as she was compelled to trust Luke.

Was there something going on between Lorna and Andrew McKennon? Not McKennon, she reminded herself. Trudeau.

A touch of sparks? She lowered her head. If so, it would be good for Lorna. But the situation itself was still frightening. Very frightening.

"I doubt that it can really be an adventure," she murmured skeptically.

Andrew hesitated. "The state needs Lorna. And Lorna needs the state."

"I understand that."

"Witnesses often become victims in one way or another."

"I . . . know."

"Donna," Luke said, "as soon as it is at all feasible, you'll be able to see her."

Donna drew in an only slightly shaky breath. "Okay. I'm not going to ask any more questions. I won't do any more snooping around. I won't do anything to risk Lorna's life or your case. But I'm not going to be able to stop worrying, and I do want to know the second that anything happens."

"You've got it," Andrew assured her.

"Thank you," Donna said. Andrew was reassuring. There was something about him despite his shaggy appearance—an air of complete authority coupled with a strange tension that very much resembled his brother's.

They made you feel safe, as if they were always aware of every sight, sound, and movement near them. Intense, concerned. Men of steel, she thought a little hysterically. But no, Superman was a myth. A comic-strip character. Luke and Andrew were real. They could be hurt. But they were also a rare breed of men. They would never step aside dispassionately when something was wrong. And if they brought you into danger, they would protect you to their last breath.

Lorna would be all right. She had to believe it, and she did. She believed in Andrew.

"—can't do that, Andrew, and you know it. The evidence would be inadmissible in court, and he'd go scot-free."

Donna gave herself a little shake. She had been so engrossed in her thoughts that she had blocked out their conversation, and now she was desperately wondering what they were talking about.

"I know," Andrew said, acknowledging his brother's words. "And that's just the point. The D.A. wants an ironclad case."

"What are you talking about?" Donna asked.

Andrew laughed. "I was thinking about some illegal breaking and entry, but my brother reminded me that in the long run, it might mean disaster." He stood up, reaching a hand out to Donna once again. "Donna, thank you."

Donna mechanically stood and accepted his hand. "I should probably be thanking you," she murmured. "But, Andrew, please—"

"I know, I know," he told her with a grin. "Don't let anything happen to Lorna. I won't. And I'll do my very best to get it all over with as soon as possible. I'll keep in touch. And with any luck, you'll be in touch with Lorna very soon."

She managed a weak smile. He released her hand and turned to his brother. "Night, Luke."

"Want to go through the front door?" Luke asked dryly.

"No, I don't want anyone associating the two of us. And besides"—he grinned very attractively—"I'm used to coming and going through the window. I'd hate to lose my finesse, you know."

He left—through the window.

And Donna was left alone with Luke, in a horrible tangle of emotions. She was still worried about Lorna. The situation was too serious for her to be anything else. And yet she felt good about her friend, better than she had in a long, long time. Andrew had given her that feeling, because if he was the one looking out for Lorna, then she just had to be okay.

"Are you all right?"

Donna realized that she had been staring out the window after Andrew. She turned to Luke. He was leaned against a corner of his desk, his arms casually crossed over his chest.

"Ah . . . yes, I guess so. I'm a little overwhelmed." Overwhelmed, overawed, and overpowered, she added silently. She would never dream of fighting the both of them on any issue. The battle would be over before it began.

Luke shrugged, but his expression was pensive. "Come on," he told her. "I'll take you back to your hotel."

"I'm sure I can get back—"

"But you know that I won't let you go alone."

Yes, she did, but she argued anyway. "Luke, I don't understand what you're worried about now. If this man Simson staged all the robberies to get away with murder, why would he keep going now—when he's already managed his murder?"

He was very still. His lashes fell, shielding the green and gold fire of his eyes. "It isn't really over yet," he told her. "Not while Simson is still walking around." He turned away from her and picked up the phone to call for a cab. Donna stood there numbly awaiting him. When he set the receiver down, his expression had changed again. Half amused. Half serious.

"What are you going to do?" he asked her.

"I—I don't know," she replied, floundering. "Wait, I guess."

"You're going to stay in New York."

"That's not exactly what I meant. It seems rather pointless for me to stay here especially now that Andrew has promised to keep in touch and let me know when it's safe to see Lorna."

"Don't you think you should stay awhile?"

"Why?" Did the question sound as breathless as she felt? And what was the answer that she wanted? He made her feel that she should run, as far and as fast as she could. But even as she decided that she should, she was longing to reach out and touch him. To allow her fingertips to study the strong planes and angles of his face and search out the mystery of his charisma. She wanted to feel the rough velvet of his palms against her cheek, the warmth and sensual magic of his mouth. . . .

"Why?" He raised a brow. "We both know, don't we? Us, Donna. You and I."

"I—I'm afraid—"

"Of me?" He asked her tensely.

She shook her head. "No," she murmured hoarsely. "Of the feeling."

He came to her then and caught her face between his hands. His eyes with all their power and magnetism stared probingly into hers. "If I were doctor, lawyer, or Indian chief, would it be different?"

"Yes," she whispered honestly.

"Give it a chance, Donna," he entreated huskily.

She nodded and when she managed to speak, she was still whispering. "I still don't really know anything about you, Luke."

He smiled and asked her, "Do you ever listen to music?"

"Ah . . . yes . . ." she murmured, trying to follow the abrupt change of conversation while lost in the mesmerization of his heated gaze and touch.

"There's a song out now. I don't know who wrote it, but Bette Midler sings it on one of her albums. I don't recall the words exactly, but it's rather fitting. Something like, 'I may not know much, but I do know that I love you.' And that might be all that anyone ever needs to know."

"Love you": He had used those words exactly. Beautiful words, encompassing her. And it was true. It was just there. The feeling. But was it enough?

"I don't know," she whispered.

"Then stay in New York awhile and find out."

"But I'm still afraid of the feeling. Of being—"

He chuckled huskily. "Donna, we'll go to the zoo, to the park, to the theater. I'll keep my hands off you." He shrugged dryly. "It will be like forty days of temptation, but I'll manage."

She found herself laughing nervously. "Fourteen days is all I can stay, Luke. I'll have to go back to Massachusetts then, for a while at least. The fiscal year will be ending and they'll need me."

"That sounds fair," he told her. Then, in a voice deep and low and that made her heart quiver, he said, "Come on. Let me get you out of here before I break my vow."

In the cab it occurred to her that she could question him, if she chose. He had been the one to say that he loved her, that she could take the time to get to know him.

"Luke?" she asked quietly, aware of the taxi driver. "What happened to your wife?"

The back of the taxi was suddenly and conveniently cast into shadow, but she felt the tension seep into his body. And for a minute she was very frightened of him.

"She died," he said harshly.

"Of what?" Donna persisted, refusing to lose her nerve.

Again he was silent for a long moment. "Cerebral hemorrhage," he said brusquely, then added, "My turn. What happened to your marriage?"

She blinked, taken aback by the abrupt turnabout. "It was annulled," she told him.

"Annulled?"

She couldn't help but smile a little dryly, a little sadly, a little bitterly. "I told you my family is very, very Catholic. When I knew that it was over, it didn't matter terribly to me how it ended but it did matter terribly to my family. So I filed for an annulment, and it was granted."

"What went wrong with the marriage?"

Donna met his eyes levelly, aware that although he was cloaked in shadow, she was bathed in a streak of light from a neon sign. "I was very much in love with my husband. He is a charming man. Nice, bright, easy to live with."

"Then?"

"He was too charming." Donna laughed. "I believe that he loved me, it just wasn't enough for him. One month into it, I found out that he was still keeping half of his clothing at another woman's apartment. He told me he'd try to leave her but he couldn't." Donna grimaced. "It hurt terribly at first. I think I spent a solid week crying and trying to find friends who would assure me that he could change. Then he told me that he had broken off with her, that it was really me whom he loved. But the next week, he was out again until three A.M. I knew then that he would never really leave me; he liked the security of marriage. I could have him but be miserable all my life. He would always be back, but he would always be gone again. I didn't want to spend my life like that—crying for sympathy, knowing inside that things would never be right. And so I left him." She smiled again. "And I really do believe Mark did love me in his way, because he didn't fight the annulment. He knew how much it meant to me."

He didn't say anything to her; he just squeezed her hand.

When they reached the Plaza, he kissed her chastely on the forehead, told her to lock her door, and walked away.

Donna lay awake half the night. She felt as if she were on fire, alive with electric currents of excitement that wouldn't allow her to sleep.

She was sure that she was falling in love but there was something a little dark and a little scary about it. She sensed that he was hiding things from her, but the longing surpassed the fear.

She spent a lot of time reminding herself that she should still be worrying about Lorna. And she was worried. But Lorna had Andrew looking after her, and that somehow made things better. It relieved her of the responsibility in a way. She couldn't do anything, except shiver with fear when she thought about the situation. And it was so easy to combat that shivering with warm and heated thoughts about Luke. Sexy thoughts. Very sexy. But it was all right to have them now. . . .

She didn't see him on Monday, but on Tuesday they went to the zoo. Tuesday night to the theater. Wednesday they took a helicopter ride around Manhattan.

On Friday, she met the three other priests who were assigned to St. Philip's—Fathers Frank, Jaime, and Paddy—when Luke invited them over for coffee. She learned that his house really wasn't the rectory—there was another building by the church that was the *real* rectory—but that Luke used his house for church purposes so frequently that it was called "Luke's rectory." Donna was intrigued by his associate fathers. The first two were young men in their twenties; both married and, like Luke, very personable. The third man—Father Paddy—was a delightful older man, enjoying duty at St. Philip's because the "youngsters," as he called the others, kept his workload low. All three men were wonderful to Donna.

Luke spoke freely to her, but she still kept that uneasy suspicion that she was seeing only the tip of the iceberg. Over lunch on Saturday she asked him to explain about his house, and it seemed that he chewed a piece of a sandwich for a long, long time before answering her.

"What we call the 'real' rectory is comprised of offices, storerooms, and the like. Paddy lives there. He has a little studio with a kitchenette fixed up. The rest of us all have our own homes—I was able to buy one near the church. I guess I have to admit to you, though, that my door, though locked, is always open. Does that bother you?"

Donna shook her head. "No, I like it," she whispered. She had come upon him that morning when his "open-door" policy had been in effect She heard him talking to a young man who had apparently run away from home. There had been no patronizing, no answer so simple as "pray for guidance, son." Luke had bluntly outlined the world for the boy. It was fine to be young, but not stupid. To err was human, but "to continue to wreck his own life was idiocy," Luke had said.

Then there were softer words, words she didn't catch. But when she had seen Luke, she had been thrilled by him all over again because she had felt such a pride in him. He didn't have to try, he didn't have to practice any techniques. He was just himself, and he brought people flocking to him. And for the first time, she had seen how very right it was for him to be a priest.

But now she was suddenly more interested in his house. "How does a priest afford such a place?"

He hesitated only briefly, then shrugged, laughing. "My family is disgustingly wealthy."

But then he changed the subject again, away from himself.

"Why don't you ever let me ask you questions?" she asked him with dismay.

"Because asking questions won't tell you what you need to know," he told her briefly.

On Sunday night, he just appeared at her door, smiling. "I've got something for you," he told her.

"What?"

"He handed her an envelope. Her heart began to thump

89

wildly when she saw her name written in Lorna's beautiful, flourishing script.

"Oh, Luke, thank you!" She cried out, impulsively hugging him. She ripped open the note and read quickly.

Donna,

I should have known you would come! Bless you, you are a love for caring, and I'm so very grateful to have you for a friend.

But I feel terrible for being so stupid too! I could have put you in danger. Well, I get bored something awful now and then, but I'm really fine—and anxious to see you soon.

All my love,
Lorna

"Oh, Luke!" Donna threw herself into his arms again, forgetting that he had promised not to touch her. Then everything that happened was natural. He was kissing her deeply, like a man who thirsted for knowledge and was determined to have it. She was able to touch him as she longed to, running her fingers over his face, entwining them in his hair, running them over the rippling muscles of his back and shoulders.

Her body seemed to change as he held her, to soften, to mold to his. The fire of his eyes was inside her, burning low, engulfing her. She knew a need for him so fierce that her mind seemed to crystallize, to fly away with his windswept touch. She tasted his teeth with her tongue, sought hungrily to have all his mouth, his lips, his scent and his taste.

"Donna . . ."

She heard her name whispered against her lips, a silken breath against her throat. Then she was moaning his, a sound that caught in her throat, becoming a whimper.

At some point they reached the bed. He was lying beside her, and his lips were fused to hers again, igniting that explosive fire. Her body changed again. It was vibrant, quivering as he touched her breast. Cupping it, skimming the nipple to a hard peak of arousal and drawing again moans that were muffled cries of his name from her lips. It was enough and she knew she loved him. . . .

His hand slipped beneath her blouse and touched her flesh. It was a touch like no other she had ever known. Hot . . . so hot . . . and so good, she could have wept with the pleasure of it. She felt his length against her, and she knew his desire. She wanted him to go on and on to love her, to give her the heights of ecstasy. He was very much a man, one who could make love with a passion and strength that would create the wildest beauty imaginable.

But suddenly it was wrong because of her life, of all the years of a priest being taboo, of not knowing if she had the strength to be the woman he could love. Because . . . she didn't really know. There were secrets. Dark mysteries. He was a man of God, but like a devil he could compel and hold, and his power over her was frightening.

She did love him, she thought with a twisting pain that knifed through her like a razor. But suddenly she was crying out his name again, and fighting his strength, and his kiss. "Luke! No!"

At the sound of her anguished voice, he released her. Shaking, Donna rolled away from him, and stared at him.

There was anger in his eyes, controlled anger, tempered with a frown of confusion. "What is it?" he asked her quietly.

"Luke—there's something about you .hat I—I don't understand," Donna stammered.

"What!" he demanded. "Are we back to the priest bit?" Sitting up, he raked his fingers through his hair. "Donna, I think you're trying real hard to turn me into a saint."

She shook her head miserably. "That's not even it," she murmured.

"Then what?"

"I still don't really know you. I don't think that many people do. Maybe I will—soon. But it's going so fast. . . ."

He sighed, "Donna, I would have stopped . . . oh, never mind." He stood up, no longer angry. "I'm really not such a mystery. And maybe . . . maybe I'm a little afraid of you too." He touched the silken locks of hair that were tumbling over her forehead in disarray. "I've got to get back tonight. Want to have dinner tomorrow?"

Donna nodded mutely. He offered her a vague smile, collected his coat, and walked to the door.

"Luke?"

He turned around.

"At dinner . . . will you answer some questions for me?"

His smile became an amused grin. "Sure."

"Promise me, Luke, please?"

"Scout's honor."

"Luke!"

"All right, all right—I swear to God!"

"Very amusing!"

"Donna, just what do you want?"

She lowered her lashes. "You," she whispered honestly. "I'm just not sure I know how to have you."

She felt his eyes on her but she couldn't look up. "I love you, Donna," he said softly, then she heard the door click quietly closed.

92

CHAPTER NINE

Luke arrived at her hotel room door at exactly seven. Donna had been ready for a long time. When his knock came, she grabbed her jacket and purse and slid outside the door quickly, before he could enter. If he noticed her somewhat panicked behavior, he didn't comment on it.

But she was sure he noticed. He had that knowing gleam to his eyes, and his lips were set in a small, almost secretive smile. She definitely amused him, but at least he wasn't rude enough to comment on it this evening.

"Where are we going?" she asked him quickly, huffing a little as she kept up with his long strides down the hallway.

"A place I think you'll like," he told her.

The elevator opened for them, and he ushered her in. It was crowded, and she had the choice of squeezing closely against him or squeezing against a very pregnant young woman in a plush sable fur. She was sure she'd sneeze all over the sable. So she crowded as close as she could to Luke. He glanced down at her, offered her a little grin, and slipped an arm about her shoulders to pull her against him.

She couldn't deny that it made her happy to be with him, to have his arm about her, to breathe his pleasant scent, feel the warmth and wiry strength of his body. And he was so incredibly good-looking. Tonight he was wearing dark trousers and a beige kidskin jacket. Soft. Nice to touch. It had that enticing smell of new leather, and the feel of it against her cheek when she was tempted to rest her head against it was wonderfully sensual.

Donna took a shaky breath as the elevator slid to a smooth halt. Everyone bustled out. His arm remained around her as he led her to the main doors and managed to efficiently charm the doorman into acquiring them a taxi instantly.

"What's the name of the restaurant?" Donna asked when she was seated next to him and the cab jerked into what she considered to be a too-speedy action.

"Caro's."

"Italian?"

"Of course," he murmured, brushing her knuckles with a light kiss that fired her entire body with a disturbing heat. "Where else does one take a gorgeous Italian?"

Donna laughed. "Am I gorgeous?"

"Beyond a doubt," he told her softly.

She turned away from him and stared at the city buildings through the neon glow of nighttime. She wanted him, cared for him, and liked him but she barely knew him. She liked his teasing banter. She liked him as a man, she was often shocked by him, but she respected his stands. And what was between them was honest; it was real. He liked her, cared for her, wanted her. She felt very feminine in his company, very much a woman.

But where did they go from there? He was a priest. To someone else, it might mean nothing. For Donna, it was a lot to handle. All of her life, a priest had been a man sworn to God—never to be thought of as a *man*. Even though he was a Protestant—and she could accept it all on a *rational* level—she still felt . . . strange. And her family! She could just imagine walking into the old triple decker house and announcing that she was in love with a Protestant priest!

The cab came to an abrupt halt. Luke helped her out, paid the driver, and started leading her along the sidewalk. All she could see before her was a gaping hole in the ground before them.

"I've got it," she teased him. "We're having dinner at a hot-dog stand in the subway."

"No," he answered calmly.

"Then we took a cab just to get to a different subway station?"

"No!" He laughed this time. "The restaurant is down those steps."

"Oh," Donna murmured uncertainly. He gave her shoulders

a little squeeze of reassurance, but Donna was still convinced that the place had to be something Andrew had stumbled on when he was slumming in the underworld.

After they descended the murky stairway, she discovered the restaurant was very nice. The lighting was subdued. Candlelight flickered from all the tables and intimate booths. A guitar was strummed lightly, and somewhere a tenor was singing Italian love songs.

"Great place for a seduction," Luke whispered to her, before greeting the maitre d'.

Yes, it was, Donna thought as they were led along a weaving path through the tables. A great place for a seduction scene. . . .

They were seated at a booth, facing one another. Bread and small dishes of antipasto had already been served. Luke raised his glass of burgundy to her. She eyed him suspiciously, but raised her glass to his.

"All right, Luke," she murmured. "You promised you would do some talking."

"Yes, I did promise, didn't I?"

"Umm-hmmm. So start talking."

"Where would you like me to start?"

"When did you decide to become a priest?"

"In the service. I was in the marines."

Donna idly picked a black olive off her plate and chewed it, grateful that the pit had been removed. "Are you going to make me drag out all the answers?"

Luke chuckled softly, then took a reflective sip of his wine. "No, I won't make you drag things out." He smiled. "I went to Catholic schools myself, you see—"

"Roman Catholic?"

He laughed. "Yes. My parents sent us all to private schools, and the best school around was run by a group of Franciscan brothers. You don't have to be Catholic to go to Catholic schools. Didn't you know that?"

"I guess I never thought about it," Donna admitted. "But," she added, "neither does going to a Catholic school automatically make one a priest—especially not an Episcopalian priest!"

Luke chuckled. "No. But I think that my interest in theology was born there. My dad, who was Church of England all the

95

way, was a great friend of one of my teachers, Brother Clement. They used to have great debates down in the cellar each winter. They'd argue until you'd think the roof was going to blow, but they always ended by deciding that God, in his infinite wisdom, came to different men in different ways."

"Then they were really very open-minded," Donna said.

"Oh, I don't know. They could take a single line from the Bible and argue over it for nights on end."

"And you—let's get back to school. Were you a model student?"

"Far from it." He grinned, his green-gold eyes a firebrand of mischief. "I think that my mother was despairing of me. I was continually on the carpet for something. I straightened up somewhat in college, worked awhile, and then I wound up in the marines."

He paused suddenly, and Donna realized that the story was about to become more serious."

"Go on, please," she prodded softly.

He shrugged, sipping his wine again. "I'd always believed in God—Dad and Father Clement, for all their differences, had thoroughly convinced me that there was a Supreme Being—and I guess that Nam was a good place to have that belief. Of course I wasn't very sure at that time that God was terribly fond of me. Anyway, we were on maneuvers one day when a buddy of mine got badly shot up. We were out in the rice paddies in the middle of nowhere. I couldn't get any help for him; all that I could do was stay with him. And I knew that he was going to die." He paused again.

"He didn't have much of a torso left," Luke said quietly. He smiled at her, a little sadly, a little ruefully. "I'll never forget it. You see, the worst of it was that Joe didn't go quickly. I can remember the day going from a blood-red sunset to a dark and humid dusk. Joe lost consciousness, then regained it. He was in a lot of pain, and wandering. I wondered if I wouldn't be doing the right thing just to kill him myself, to rid him of his pain. But I didn't. I think we all like to believe in miracles.

"Anyway, Joe started to believe that I was his priest. He wanted me to pray for him. So I started trying to pray. And here I was with this poor man, stuttering out some words. And all I could think was that Joe had the worst representative in the world going for him. I thought about all the sins in my undistinguished life, and my tears were falling all over Joe because I felt so helpless—and so sure that God would never listen to a word that I had to say. But I had to try. I had to help Joe somehow. So I turned away and literally slapped myself. I turned back to him and assured him that I was his priest. I started praying again, all the nice things I remembered from all those mornings in mass. And suddenly Joe stopped screaming. He was relaxed, no longer frightened."

Donna felt a little chill seep through her. She moistened her lips to speak, but the sound was still a whisper.

"Joe lived?"

Luke smiled, shaking his head. "No, I'm not a miracle worker. But somehow . . . I don't really know how to say this. He—he died easily. Almost smiling. As if he had entered a far better world. Maybe it was the last illusion of an agonized man, but it was as if he knew he was about to reach heaven. But right before he died, he opened his eyes and stared straight at me. And he said, 'Thank you, Luke. God bless you, son.'"

"And you decided then to be a priest?"

"No, not exactly. It wasn't one of those instant decisions. But it was a long night. I just sat there, holding Joe's body, for what seemed like forever. It took until morning for the rest of the patrol to find us. I don't know, I guess I started thinking then that my life really hadn't been worth much of anything to anyone. And it might very well have been me rather than Joe who died. When I got back to base, I guess I was in shock. Father McKay—who is a Roman Catholic, by the way—spent a lot of time with me. He suggested that I'd be a perfect candidate for the priesthood. I told him he was crazy. But I'd begun to wonder. . . . Then I told him again that he was absolutely crazy because if I was going to do something, I'd want to do it right. And I was opinionated, temperamental—et cetera. McKay knew I was an Episcopalian, but our unit didn't have an Episcopalian priest at that time. So he waited, and then as we moved closer to base, he went in and found Father Austin—a very young man, by the way—who was an Episcopalian. Austin and I became good friends. He tried not to influence me—he just answered questions. And he played a great game of tin can putt-putt."

Luke hesitated. "I still wasn't sure when I got back to the States, but I entered a seminary and I came out a priest."

He stopped speaking, smiling as the waiter appeared with large plates of lasagna.

"The best you'll ever taste!" the waiter assured them before hurrying away. Luke and Donna both remained silent as they bit into their food.

"Well?" Luke asked her.

"Well?"

"Is it the best you've ever tasted?"

"It's very, very good," Donna replied, smiling. "But I'm afraid my grandmother still makes the absolute best I've ever tasted."

He reached across the table and she felt the feather-light caress of his fingers over her hand. "I'd just love to taste your grandmother's lasagna, you know."

Donna flushed slightly. Oh, no, she thought. She wasn't so sure that he would because it would be served in the midst of pure chaos, with her grandfather there like a reigning monarch. And he'd probably drive Luke to murder because to him, anyone who isn't Italian isn't civilized, and anyone who isn't Catholic is a pagan.

But she didn't withdraw her fingers. She smiled weakly and changed the subject. "I'd like to ask you something else," she told him.

"Shoot."

Did he mean it? She could have sworn a thin veil of wariness had descended darkly over the golden glitter in his eyes. They seemed to say ask . . . ask all the questions you like and I'll answer them, exactly as I choose. . . .

Donna hesitated. She set down her fork and at last withdrew her fingers from his, folding her hands in her lap. Then she grimaced. "When I wasn't worried about the fires of hell and eternal damnation for the way I was feeling about you, I was . . . uh . . . worried about something else."

"Oh?" He arched one of his brows high. Donna decided that he was still very capable of looking diabolical. The devil's own, sinfully attractive temptation.

"Yes," she murmured, and then she laughed. "Luke, I don't know how to say this, but I feel there's something about you that I don't know. That . . . oh, I don't know. I saw all those books in your study about E.S.P. and the occult—"

He smiled, lowering his head quickly. Then his eyes raised to hers, filled with mischief once again. "I see. You had me performing virgin sacrifices upon the altar and worshipping an inverted cross?"

Donna blushed. "No!"

"I'm relieved, although I'm quite sure you'd make a gorgeous sacrifice. The largest library on the occult in the world is at the Vatican, you know. A lot of it is reading material that any student of theology should read."

"I know, I know. That's not what I mean."

"Then what do you mean?"

"I just feel that you're . . . a lot deeper than I'll ever know," she finished lamely.

"Aren't we all?" he replied lightly. "I imagine, Donna Miro, that you're a deep lady yourself."

"Not at all the same way," she murmured, lowering her lashes again, flushing. The way he was looking at her. . . . "Luke . . ." Her voice was incredibly husky. She sipped her wine so quickly that it dribbled down her chin, and she was fumbling for her napkin, flushing with embarrassment. But her napkin never reached her chin. He reached across the table again in a fluid and natural movement. He touched her chin with his finger, catching the wine. Then he grazed that finger over her lips, following its path with his eyes. It was a slightly rough touch. His fingertips were calloused. But it was tender and gentle, and it suddenly made her shiver despite the hot flash of desire that engulfed her. His lips curved into a wistful smile, and his voice was as husky as hers.

"I wish I could look at you with that wine on your lips and dribbling down your chin and think that you were a klutz. Instead I look at you and think that I'd like to take the full glass of wine and dribble it all over your body and then taste it."

"Luke!" Donna gasped, and she knew that the color of her cheeks could be no lighter than the tomato sauce in the lasagna.

He chuckled and regretfully settled back into his side of the booth, removing his touch. She felt horribly bereft and a little bit ashamed of herself, because it was so easy to follow his line of thought—imagining the two of them together with a whole cask of wine to kiss from one another's flesh.

"I've told you how I feel," he said with a touch of amusement along with the sound of a sigh.

"I—I just can't seem to get accustomed to the idea of a priest . . ."

"Being lascivious?" He offered.

"Exactly," she replied, laughing nervously.

He smiled. "We're not doing much justice to this lasagna."

"You've ruined my appetite," Donna accused him.

"I'm sorry. That was never my intent."

"You have my stomach in knots."

He leaned close to her once again, arching a satanic brow. "Ah, that's exactly how you're supposed to feel. Quivery . . . confused. Hot one moment, riddled with chills the next. And very, very hungry . . . but not for food."

"And if I do feel like that," she whispered, unable to resist the temptation to reach out and brush her knuckles against the masculine texture of his freshly shaven cheek, "what do I do?"

"You come to me, and I put my arms around you . . . and you just trust me to take it from there."

She chuckled again uncertainly. "Luke, I like you. You know that. It's just so new, and I still feel so very unsure. . . ."

He took her hand again, lightly, between both of his. "I understand that," he told her softly.

"So what do we do?" she whispered, aware that the question was a beseechment.

"I could turn into a mad rapist," he offered.

Donna pursed her lips in a wry smile and lowered her eyes. "I don't think that would be in character."

"You don't? Watch out, then, Ms. Miro. Dark secrets lurk in the hearts of the best of men. Umm . . . what do we do? I might be an unorthodox priest, but I am one. I think that I'm falling in love with you. That means a lot of things. It means I want you. To hold you, and to love. And more. It would mean marriage. To have and to hold, et cetera, until death."

"I know," she whispered.

"And?"

"It frightens me."

He smiled. "I'd be insulted if it didn't."

Donna returned his smile, but weakly. "I'm not sure we know one another well enough for this discussion."

"We can keep getting to know one another."

Donna's smile became suddenly strong and sincere. "That may be difficult. Haven't you realized that I'm afraid to be alone with you?"

"Yes, as a matter of fact, I have. But I don't intend to let it stand in my way. You can keep trying to slip by me, and I can make sure that you don't always succeed."

"That's just what I'm afraid of."

"But you won't be. Because once I have you, I'll try very hard to see that you aren't thinking at all."

"Not a mad rapist, just a mad seducer?"

"Half seducer. Just enough to convince you that I am a man, very capable of loving a woman."

"Oh," Donna murmured, finding safety in turning her attention back to her lasagna, "I never doubted your capabilities."

He allowed it to rest at that and took a bite of his meal.

Donna suddenly stared at him again. "You managed to evade my question," she accused him.

"I did?" He asked innocently.

Or was it so innocent? Did a wary shield once again cloud the golden warmth of his eyes.

"I said that I think that you're hiding something from me."

"Like what?"

"I don't know."

"Then maybe there isn't anything to know."

He smiled, as if teasing her. Perhaps she deserved it.

"Okay, Luke, I'll let that pass—for now."

He sighed, setting down his fork. "Donna, if you're still referring to my books, I read a lot of things. I like to read. And I teach a class each spring at Columbia on theology. A nonsecular class. We go back to the roots of man, superstition, and all that. Are you satisfied?"

She nodded but wondered at the sudden edge to his voice. "Did you major in theology at college yourself?" she asked him.

"No, theology was my minor."

"What was your major?" She queried, very curious.

The edge left his voice as he laughed. "Criminal law. My mother was dying to have a son become an F. Lee Bailey."

"Law?"

"Yes. I passed the bar and I practiced for a year, but then I wound up in the marines, and after the marines—well, you know that story. I studied theology—and kept up with the law —at the seminary. And now, well, I teach a few law classes at Columbia too. Only in the spring." He grinned. "God can be a very demanding employer. I teach only in the spring, because it's the season when I'm given an extra man from the seminary."

"You're very irreverent for a priest," Donna told him.

"That, Ms. Miro, is a point I could debate with you all evening."

"I'm sure you could." Donna pushed her dish away; she simply couldn't eat any more. She frowned suddenly. "Luke, what about your family?"

"What about them? You've met Andrew." He said it dryly, but she felt a little warmed by the affection in his voice for his brother.

"Is it just the two of you?" She asked.

"No, I have two sisters. And my mother and father, of course."

"What do they think of you being a priest?"

Luke, too, pushed his plate aside. He leaned back in the booth as he lit a cigarette. "Cappuccino?" He asked her. "It's excellent here."

She nodded. He raised two fingers to the waiter, and Donna decided he was well known there. Their plates were taken away, and two cups of steaming cappuccino were set before them.

"Okay," he said once the waiter had left them again. "Although I think you've had more than twenty questions answered. My mother wasn't quite certain what to think—she was worried about my temper too, I guess. But once she knew that I had made up my mind and was determined, she must have decided that it was a vocation that would keep me off the streets. I don't think that my father was ever surprised."

Donna couldn't keep her lips from twitching into a smile. "Your poor mother!" she commiserated. "And she wanted an F. Lee Bailey!"

"She may still get one."

"Oh?"

"My sister Jean is a wonderful attorney."

Donna tasted her cappuccino. It was delicious. It made her think of a warm fire in a darkened room, leaning against the man she loved in contentment. It made her think of all the very different ways she would like to be together with Luke.

"Donna."

"What?"

She gazed across at him. The laughter was gone from his eyes; so were all shields. They were sharp and demanding. He didn't touch her, he didn't lean toward her, but she felt his power of command, just as she felt his tension. He would never need to convince her that he was all male, all man.

"What we do, where we go, has to be up to you."

She nodded. She just needed more time.

She couldn't help lowering her eyes and playing with her cup. "I'm still so worried about Lorna," she murmured.

"I know. But you can't do anything."

"I know. I was thinking I should go home. I need time to think."

She thought she heard a soft sigh . . . of disappointment? But she couldn't help it, she had to be sure.

"Maybe that's the best idea," he said lightly. A moment later he was asking for the check, and then they were back out in the darkness of night. It seemed to have grown cold, Donna thought.

"Feel like walking?" he asked her.

She nodded vaguely, feeling as if she had lost something, that wonderful feeling of closeness, of being held, cherished, protected . . . loved.

They started walking down the street. Donna glanced dubiously at the buildings they passed.

"I remember you telling me not to take a cab to church by myself. Isn't it a little dangerous in this area?" Donna asked lightly.

She was relieved to feel his arm around her again. "You're shivering. Are you cold?"

"No, not really."

"Frightened?"

"I don't think so."

"Nothing will happen to you when you're with me," he told her softly.

It wasn't a long walk. Within minutes, they were skirting around Central Park. Donna felt again the way she had when she had sipped her cappuccino. It was a cool night, brisk and beautiful, wonderful to share. She stepped ahead of him suddenly, enthralled by a pile of leaves. She stooped and raked a bunch into her hands, letting them flutter and fall through her fingers with childish delight.

"Oh, Luke! Isn't it a perfect night! All the colors in the leaves." She paused, breathing in the scent of the leaves. "It smells just like fall!"

"It smells like horse manure!" He snorted. "And watch it—you're just about to step in some."

Donna carefully sidestepped the less-colorful pile on the ground. "No appreciation." She sniffed. She heard his soft, husky chuckle behind her. Soon they reached the hotel.

He opened the door to her room, but then stood aside. Donna turned back to him expectantly. He smiled at her with that warm glint of mischief burning in his eyes.

"Are . . . are you coming in?" She asked nervously.

"Actually, I was waiting for you to try to slam the door in my face."

That's exactly what she should do, Donna thought. But it had been nice, too nice, being with him. The cool weather, thoughts of winter, being together, being held. . . .

"I . . . uh . . . well, it's still rather early. They have cable movies on television here. There might be something good on."

"Why, Ms. Miro! I'm shocked. You're actually inviting me into your bedchamber."

"Ah, Father, how witty!" Donna taunted him in return. "But, alas, no. This isn't my bedchamber. It's just a hotel room. And if you do want to come in, do so quickly, before I realize how insane I'm behaving."

"Well, Ms. Miro, I wouldn't want you compromising my position, you know."

"Luke! In or out!" Donna begged.

With a devilish flash of white teeth, he stepped into the room. Donna rather nervously wandered away from him, making a

104

careful study of the program listing. "Oh, *Vacation* is on. It's cute—have you seen it?"

"Turn it on."

Donna flicked on the TV. The picture came on sketchily. Luke cast off his jacket and stepped by her to fiddle with the buttons. The picture became clearer.

"Well," she said, "I'd offer you something, but—" She lifted her hands with a gesture that indicated she was entertaining in a hotel room. Then she laughed suddenly. "But I can order something from room service. Coffee, tea, hot chocolate?"

"Donna, you don't need—"

"Oh, but I'm just dying for some hot chocolate."

Luke agreed to hot chocolate, and Donna called in the order. She realized they were both standing around. There was a single chair in the room badly situated for TV viewing.

She was falling in love with him, she reminded herself as she tried to decide whether to sit in the chair or on the bed. The bed . . . She was leaving tomorrow and she owed herself this night near him, close to him, to see whether her feelings of love died in discomfort, or grew despite everything.

She smiled at him suddenly, very wistfully. Then she kicked off her fashionable ankle boots and crawled onto the bed, sweeping a hand over the mattress at her side. "Father, will you join me?"

He chuckled, casting off his own shoes and shaking his head sardonically. "I'll join you, but only if you quit calling me Father."

Donna allowed her eyes to grow innocently wide. "But you are a 'Father,' Luke."

"Somehow the title just doesn't sound right, coming from you." He climbed on the bed beside her. "I'm glad I decided to wear matching socks," he muttered.

She smiled, and a few minutes later, it was everything that she wanted it to be. Comfortable, wonderful. They pulled the pillows to the foot of the bed and stretched out beside one another. They didn't reach out to touch each other, they didn't have to. Donna could feel the warmth radiating from the length of his body, but she didn't feel threatened. She felt as if she belonged where she was, luxuriating in his warmth, secure in his quiet strength.

The hot chocolate came, and they sipped it while commenting on the movie. Nothing serious was said, no questions were asked.

But halfway through the movie, Donna began to yawn. She felt so secure, so at peace. She wished that she could fall asleep with him there beside her. She wished that he would slip an arm around her and that she could curl against his length. . . .

"I think I'd better go," he said huskily.

He stood. His hair was somewhat rumpled, but dishevelment didn't mar his looks. It made him look more ruggedly appealing than ever. Donna felt as if her heart were skipping beats, warning her that the pain of loss was near.

But she had to go home. Things were moving too quickly for her. She was in over her head. Her emotions were rushing like a waterfall over a chasm and she could go no further unless she was sure she could ride out all of the rapids that were in her way.

He slid into his jacket then walked to her side. "Good-bye, Donna," he said softly.

He didn't touch her though she yearned for his touch.

Without looking back, he walked to the door. But he wasn't able to touch it.

"Luke!" His name tore from her with an anguished cry, and she was bounding from the bed, staring at him with hunger and torment.

He stopped, turning back to her, raising a brow in a silent and eloquent query.

"Don't—don't go," she pleaded. "Not . . . yet."

He didn't move. Donna raced across the room, catapulting into his arms. Beneath the soft kid of his jacket she felt the hardness of his arms, the granite warmth of his chest. She touched his cheek tentatively with her palm. Her eyes beseeched his.

He cupped her chin with his palm, caressing it. His mouth moved slowly to take hers, barely touching it at first. His tongue drew a silken line over her lower lip. Then his mouth fused with hers, and his hands raked into her hair, then down the length of her back, to her hips, holding her close, lifting her, closer, closer.

Sweet, burning heat. She tasted it on his lips, she felt it envelop her. His was all the colors of the autumn leaves, the texture of a midnight, rough velvet sky. He coaxed and he commanded, he crushed the breath from her, he ravaged, and yet he gave with tenderness, always feeding the fires of her own hunger and need. She felt weak against him; he shifted slightly, holding her, loving her, molding the length of her body to his so that she knew him from the taste of his tongue to the muscled strength of his thighs. She was so pliable, so willing to know him.

His lips moved from hers, returned to them again with little nibbling kisses. Kisses that roamed . . . tasted . . . savored. She felt his lips against her cheek, warm, a breath of arousal at her earlobe, touching the pulse that beat furiously in the arched column of her throat. He found her mouth again, taking it with a wild hunger that drew a moan from her muffling again into the ache of desire. Then he set her away from him, smiling with the devil's own taunt burning in the golden depths of his eyes.

"Seductress!" he teased huskily. "You could melt a heart of a stone." He chastely kissed her forehead. "But that, Ms. Miro, is all that you're going to get. Until you agree to marry me, of course."

But it wasn't all that she got. He pulled her to him again and held her. It was hard to let her go. So very hard. Especially when he held her. When he had tasted the sweetness of her sensuality. Felt the rise of passion. Her hips pressed to his. The full, rounded and firm swell of her breast, brushing his chest, tempting him as the best of saints could not be tempted and survive. He could have her but risk the chance of losing her forever. And forever was what he wanted.

"Decide quickly, Donna. Please. And come back . . . to me."

He released her and stepped swiftly from the room.

In the hallway he uttered a low groan, steadying himself against the wall. She was small . . . so petite against him. But so fully, femininely formed. Marvelous breasts. Tiny waist. Long, shapely legs, curvaceous hips, rounded derriere . . . Her eyes framed in dark, sultry lashes. Full lips, sensually sculpted, demanding to be kissed whether she laughed or frowned. She was beautiful and also one of the sexiest women he had ever met. His little Italian temptress. She had made him feel whole again.

Well, he was in a little bit of agony at the minute, but she had given him something. He felt so vital and alive . . . and in love.

When he stepped into the night again, the stars were shining. It was still cool, and still beautiful. It smelled like fall.

He stared up at the stars, and at the heavens, and he smiled.

"Thank you, Lord. Thank you for bringing her to me. And you know, I really don't ask for a lot of personal favors, but do you think that you could make this one work out? Only if it's Your Will, of course. But, do you think that you could make it Your Will?"

He whistled as he eschewed the idea of a cab and started walking once again.

New York City. She hosted the rich and the famous; she cradled the destitute and weary. Flash and neon, graffiti and crime. It had taken a heavy toll from him and daily demanded more and more. But it seemed that it had also given something back.

Donna Miro. . . .

CHAPTER TEN

It had been a long day. Donna had wrestled with the accountant all morning over fiscal year quarterly taxes, then she had spent the afternoon with the ad exec who was taking over their account. She wanted nothing more than to drive out of Worcester to her own small house in Auburn and soak in a tub of hot bubbles all night.

Donna collected her purse and sweater and moved down the hallway to the firm's largest office—her father's. She smiled at his secretary, then slipped inside.

Sal Miro had eyes as light as his daughter's and hair as dark, except that his was streaked with what Donna thought of as very dignified silver. He was a handsome man, she thought with pride. Medium height, slim build, and generally, a smile for everyone. He had been brought to the United States as a small boy, and he had embraced his new country with nothing short of reverence. Neither the long years of struggle to build the business nor the insanity in the house where he had raised, and was still raising, the last of his six children had ever damaged his sunny disposition.

He was on the phone when she entered the office, so she waited, returning his smile. But after he said good-bye, he didn't hang up the receiver. He grimaced slightly and handed it to Donna. She glanced at him questioningly. "Your grandmother," he whispered.

Donna grimaced herself and took the phone. "Hi, Gram."

"Donna, you come to dinner tonight." Her grandmother's heavily accented English made Donna smile.

"Gee, Gram, I'd love to, but—"

"No butsa! You come. I have a surprise for you."

Donna exhaled. Her grandmother—whom her father had taken after, thank God!—was surely the sweetest woman in the world. It was hard to refuse her anything. "I'm really tired, Gram."

"You don'ta eata right!"

Donna chuckled. "Gram, if I ate like you wanted me to, they'd have to roll me down the street. Listen, Gram, another night, okay? I'm really—"

"Per favore, Donna!"

"All right, all right, I'll be there! But I can't stay late!"

"Gratzie!"

The receiver went dead in Donna's hand. Her father winked at her. "You should have said yes to begin with and saved yourself some trouble."

Donna laughed and took her father's arm. "You're probably right. Grandpa hollers, but Gram just asks softly and we all jump."

"Yep—same way it's been for years," her father agreed. He stared at her as if he wanted to say something but hesitated.

"What, Dad?" She asked him.

"I'm glad she called, and I'm glad you're coming home for dinner tonight," Sal said. "You've been a little strange, honey, ever since you came home from New York. Are you sure everything is okay with Lorna?"

"Yes, I'm sure," Donna said, lowering her lashes with the lie. She had told her parents that she had learned Lorna had taken a trip to Europe.

"Something else is bothering you, isn't it?"

"No, I'm fine, just tired."

Sal chuckled, slipping an arm around his daughter's shoulders. "I see. It's a man."

Donna flushed, not really surprised by her father's perception. He was often a very quiet man, but she had learned long ago that he was quiet because he listened well and ascertained all the things said between the lines.

"Yes," she told him.

"What's the problem?" Her father's voice took on a slightly rough edge. "He's not another . . . Mark, is he?"

"No, Dad, nothing like that," Donna answered.

"You don't want to talk about it?"

Donna shrugged. Why not? she asked herself. Who better to talk to than her own father?

"He's a priest," she said a little distractedly.

"A *what?*"

For all the wild shouting that went on in her household, Donna had seldom heard her father really raise his voice.

She was certain that half of Worcester had heard him—and worse, his face had turned a mottled red. She was in sudden panic that she might have caused him a stroke.

"Not a Catholic priest, Dad!" She wailed quickly, patting him on the back. "Dad? Dad?" There was an old-fashioned silver water pitcher sitting on his desk, and a tray of glasses. She quickly poured him some water. He drank it gratefully, watching her over the rim of the glass. Donna started talking quickly. "Dad, he's an Episcopalian priest."

"An Episcopalian priest?"

"Yes, Dad."

Sal shook his head. She might as well have told him that she had been seeing a two-headed monster. He took a deep breath and smiled weakly at her. "Donna—get me some more water will you? No, on second thought, there's a bottle of blackberry brandy in my desk. Get it out, please?"

Donna did as her father shuffled around for shot glasses. He poured out two shots.

"Dad?" Donna queried nervously.

He drank down one of the shots. "I'm thinking, I'm thinking," he murmured. He picked up the other glass, drank it quickly, and stared at her.

"You're really in love with him, aren't you?"

Donna nodded.

Her father glanced at her then sighed, closed his eyes tightly, and opened them again. "This is America," he said finally. "And I always wanted to raise my children to be Americans. That means tolerance and acceptance."

"Dad, are you saying that you don't mind?"

"I mind, but I love you, Donna. And if it had been a Buddhist monk to make you happy, then I would have accepted a Buddhist monk."

"Oh, Dad!" Donna exclaimed. She wrapped her arms tightly around him. "I love you so much!"

111

He returned her hug and grimaced. "So many years, Donna, yet the family remains so close; so important. Children grow up and they leave. But your grandparents have kept us all together. I have six children, and in my heart I know that no matter how far they go, they will come back. You'll be the first to marry outside our religion, Donna. But changes come." He looked at her sharply. "Will you . . . will you convert?"

Donna shook her head. "He has never suggested it, Dad."

"An Episcopalian priest will have a Catholic wife?"

"He asks nothing of me, Dad."

Sal nodded slowly. "Don't think any more then, Donna, about what he is, or what he does. Just ask yourself if you really love him."

"I do."

"Then you have no problem."

"Thank you for that, Dad. I do, in a way, still have a problem. Gram wrote so many letters to the archbishop—and then to the Pope!—to see my annulment through. So that I could be married in the church—"

"It's . . . possible that you could be married by both churches," Sal suggested.

"Perhaps. I—I don't really know."

Sal sighed again. "Donna, your mother will say little. She will have her reservations, but she will say little. Your grandmother will also keep her thoughts to herself. You can almost count on your grandfather putting you through misery. Be kind to him, because he is an old, old man now who fought very hard for his family. But stick to your guns, Donna. You do what you feel best."

"I will, Dad. Thank you so much."

One hurdle that she had been dreading, Donna thought, was over. She could get through the rest. But she was still worried, still uncertain. And it wasn't the fact that Luke was a priest. . . .

She shook her head. She didn't know him, nor what had put that brooding look in his eyes and had bruised his heart. But marriage . . . marriage meant years of discovery. She loved Luke; she had to believe that time would give her all the rest.

Sal was staring at her strangely and she lowered her eyes again. She knew her father had never cared for Mark, but he had never said a word against him to her. Her annulment had hurt him and her mother and the rest of the family because they hurt for one another.

She was surprised when he put his arms around her and hugged her tight. "Is he in love with you?"

"I think so," she repeated.

"Be sure, honey, then do whatever you have to do."

"I will."

"At least I know now," he told her, his blue eyes twinkling like diamonds against his olive complexion, "why you've been lost in a dream world lately. You miss him."

So badly that it hurt, Donna thought, but didn't say aloud. "I kind of walked out on him," she said, then smiled as she took his arm. "Come on, Dad, I think we'll hit all the traffic if we don't hurry."

America and the olive-oil business had been good to the Miro family. They could have lived anywhere they wanted now, but they had remained in a triple decker on Shrewesbury Street. Her grandparents lived on the top floor, her parents in the middle, and her brother Vic, his wife, and two small daughters lived on the ground floor. The house was surrounded by old trees, barren now with winter almost upon them. But even when the grass had died and the leaves had fallen, there was something special about the lawn and the old triple decker. It was a welcoming place. Generations of children had lived and played and grown up there, and if love could be a tangible thing that hung in the air, it did so here.

A loud scream suddenly tore from the house, followed by a child's wail and a mother's soothing voice. "The girls are at it again," Sal said with a wink to his daughter. "But I don't think they're as wild as the bunch I raised."

She grinned, stamped her feet on the back mat, and opened the door to the rear porch. Her brother Vic's wife, Theresa, was standing there with a huge pot of sausage and peppers, trying to control a squabble between the three-year-old and the four-year-old over a new Cabbage Patch doll. "Dad . . . Donna, hi!"

Sal rescued the sausage and peppers. Theresa kissed them

113

both. "Hurry on up, you two," Theresa urged them. "Gram is waiting."

Donna had picked up her youngest niece, who lost interest in the doll as she played with Donna's gold chain.

"I'll take a moppet with me and get one out of your hair," she offered to Theresa.

Theresa grimaced, her beautiful dark eyes expressing her appreciation. "Thanks, but be warned. There are moppets all over the place tonight."

She went on to explain that two sets of aunts and uncles were coming with their children and their children's children. And Donna's other older brother, Tom, was coming with his wife, Sally, and their baby.

Donna laughed. "Thanks for the warning, but I think I can handle it. After all, I get to go home afterward!"

"I'm going up," Sal said.

"Coming, Dad," Donna answered. She started up the steps.

"Personally," Theresa called after her, laughing, "I think Gram's lost her mind, inviting him for dinner. If I were to walk into a madhouse like this for the first time, I probably wouldn't date you again no matter how gorgeous you were!" She chuckled softly, her eyes alive with affectionate teasing. "But, oh, is he gorgeous himself!"

Donna felt a sudden freeze come over her, as if winter had suddenly arrived in full. "Theresa!" she called sharply.

But the door to Theresa's ground-floor apartment had already swung shut. "What's she talking about?" Donna demanded of her father.

Sal was already several steps ahead of her, passing his own door. "I haven't the slightest idea, honey, but this pot is getting hotter by the second!"

"Walk, Auntie Donna!"

She had forgotten she was holding a moppet. She obediently began to climb again.

It couldn't be Luke, it couldn't be Luke, she hadn't heard a word from him since she had returned. She had lain awake for many nights, thinking she should pick up the phone, call him, admit that she was a confused coward, but that she was sorry, she did love him, she wanted to see him.

But she hadn't picked up the phone. She had begun to fear

that she had imagined loving him, that she had wished it to be there; he had been the sexiest, strongest, most charismatic man she had ever met and, like a fool, she had let it all slip from her grasp. She had walked away, and he had probably decided to let her go.

She had almost reached the third-level porch, and once again, she could hear voices.

"Dina, get up and getta the napkins, please."

Her grandmother was talking to Donna's younger sister.

"Tony is right there." Dina was probably reading the latest soap magazine and determined not to take her avid eyes from the written words, Donna thought, laughing to herself.

"Hey! Thunder thighs! Get up when Gram talks to you!"

Her younger brother Tony was fighting with Dina as usual.

"Shut up, knockwurst nose! You're not such a help yourself."

Donna sighed. Dina, as usual, fighting back.

Her father, with a frown of annoyance, pushed open the screen door to the huge kitchen, about to quietly reprimand his two teenagers. But Donna was right behind him, and before he could speak, she gasped loudly, distractedly setting down her little niece who crawled onto Dina's lap.

Luke was there, sitting opposite her grandfather at the small butcher-block table near the kitchen's heating stove. A bottle of anisette sat between the two; it appeared that they had been talking and exchanging shot for shot.

"Oh, Lord!" Donna groaned, barely aware that she had said the words out loud.

"Not the Lord, Donna," her grandmother, busily wiping her hands on her apron, said as she came to kiss her son and then Donna. "He's justa ni-sa priest."

Luke was standing, walking across the floor. He smiled at her, but offered his hand to her father. "Mr. Miro, I'm Luke Trudeau. Donna and I met in New York recently. I came to look her up and finagled a dinner invitation."

Sal took his hand. Donna barely heard her father welcoming him. She was trembling, thinking that she had just walked in and the house was already in chaos.

Luke's eyes met hers, gold, tender, amused. He looked wonderful and so tall that he filled the small kitchen, so handsome

115

that Donna realized it hadn't been a soap magazine enthralling Dina, but Luke.

Suddenly she smiled, glad to see him. He wouldn't mind the chaos. He would accept it and love it, because he loved her.

She laughed and reached out her own hand. "Hello, Luke," she said softly, huskily. She inclined her head toward her still-squabbling siblings. "I see you've already met Thunder Thighs and Knockwurst Nose."

Luke chuckled that low sound that could touch and entice her so easily. "Yes, I have. And your mother, your grandfather and grandmother. Your brother, sister-in-law, and nieces. Your cousin Janice and—"

"Donna!" Her grandmother's voice, calling her, interrupted a list that might have been—if he'd met only half of her family—endless.

"Donna, I needa some bread. Be a gooda girl and run to the corner for me, yes?"

Donna looked curiously at her grandmother beyond Luke's broad shoulders. There was never a lack of bread in the house. Her grandfather went to the corner bakery every morning, rain, snow, or shine.

She was stunned to see her grandmother wink. She grinned broadly. "Sure, Gram, I'll go."

"Give your grandfather a kiss and say hello to your mother first."

She cast Luke a quick glance to excuse herself and hurried to her grandfather, planting a kiss on his snow-white head. She hurried past him, to the dining room beyond the kitchen, and found her mother setting the table.

"Hi, Mom," she said, giving out another quick kiss and a hug.

"Donna!" her mother exclaimed happily, setting down her load of silverware to make the hug longer than Donna had intended. Then she set her daughter from her to study her anxiously.

Donna laughed. Her mother was one of the prettiest women she knew. Small, sweet—and plump. She was continually dieting, but she lived in a den of temptation. She was, however, the only one who considered herself to be overweight. Donna had often heard her father say that her mother's full curves were his

116

most cherished possessions. She was only two inches taller than her mother, and prone to the same full curves. Only by living away from home had she managed to keep the pounds off.

Her mother also had the most expressive eyes Donna had ever seen, and right now they were expressing a large amount of anxiety. "Honey, who is this man?"

"Luke?" Donna stalled, ridiculously.

"He's a priest," her mother said.

"I know."

"Why is he here? Did you have trouble in New York?"

Donna shook her head. "He's a friend, Mother."

"He's not Catholic, is he?"

"No, Mom."

"He's not even Italian."

Donna started to laugh. "Not everyone is, Mom."

Her mother turned and retrieved the silverware. She continued to arrange place settings, glancing nervously at the door to see that they weren't interrupted. She stopped again, setting the silverware down and putting her hands on her hips.

"I think your grandfather was about to have a stroke when he came in and introduced himself. The next thing I know, he's got the anisette open, and your friend has him purring like a kitten." She shook her head quizzically, looking at Donna. Then she shrugged. "He must be the beloved of God to have gotten past your grandfather!"

The words were said so seriously, with such conviction, that Donna forced herself to conceal the laughter that bubbled within her. "Luke does have a way with people, Mom."

"With you too, huh?"

"Yes, Mom."

"He's a nice-looking man. A very nice-looking man." Her mother looked down suddenly, straightening the very straight table cloth. "I—I'm not sure I like nice-looking young men." She hesitated. "Your Mark, honey, he was nice-looking too. Not like this . . . but . . ."

"Mom!" Donna moaned. "I haven't judged all men by Mark. Please, don't you start doing so because of me. Luke is a . . . priest. I don't think that priests are known for running around on their—" She paused. She had almost said wives. "They're

117

not known for running around. But, Mom, no matter what Luke did, I would trust him. He's that kind of man."

Her mother looked at her, and Donna was surprised at the relief she saw in her mother's eyes. "Donna, I like him. Yes, I think I like him very much. But"—she took a step closer—"watch out for your grandfather. I don't think that he's realized yet that this priest has come for his granddaughter!"

Donna smiled. "I'll watch out, Mom. Thanks."

Just as she heard the words, another squabble broke out. Thunder Thighs and Knockwurst Nose were at it again. And then her grandfather's voice—rising high. His rebukes poured out half in English and half in Italian.

"I'll be back, Mom," Donna said nervously. "I'm going to take Luke for a walk to pick up some bread."

"Bread?" Her mother inquired in confusion. "But, honey, we don't need any bread—"

"I know. But Gram is right on the ball."

She was glad to see her mother grin. "She certainly is. She would have to be to live with your grandfather all these years!"

Donna eluded her grandfather on the way out, snatching Luke quickly from his post between her sister and Vic, who had just come up. She clutched his hand and practically dragged him down the stairs. Not until they were halfway down the street did she pause, turn to him to see the confusion on his face, and burst into laughter.

"Oh, Luke! What are you doing here? How long have you been here? How have you stood being here? Luke—"

She flung her arms around his neck suddenly, pressing her body to the length of his and hugging him. Mindless of where she stood, she stretched up on tiptoe and planted hurried kisses against his cheeks and then his lips in a burst of hunger and longing.

"I missed you so much," she murmured, suddenly growing shy and burying her face against his coat.

He lifted her chin. She met the green and gold fire in his eyes, the promise that he hadn't lost his passion or need for her. "I had to come," he told her huskily. His lips found hers again, warm and sure and hinting of things restrained that could engulf them both in the middle of the street. His scent wrapped her in a sweet rapture as did the radiating heat of his body, the feel of his arms, strong and secure about her.

His lips left hers too soon. But they stayed close. So close that she could breathe his whisper and quiver with the anticipation of his touch.

"Are you going to marry me?" he asked her.

She nodded. His mouth claimed hers once more, parting it, plundering it, tongues meeting in a sweet and breathless duel. But when they broke again and Donna searched out his eyes, she realized that she had made an unspoken commitment to him. Total commitment. She knew how very badly she wanted him, but she also knew that marriage with him would be a tempest, one from which she could not retreat. Quivers touched her spine and a strange burning touched her belly. Yes, she wanted him. She loved him. But a lot about him still seemed to be a mystery. Dark secrets, hidden from her. . . .

"I—I want to marry you, Luke. But I still think that we have to wait."

"Are you afraid of your family?"

She shook her head. "No. Well, maybe, yes, a little. Only my grandfather. You've heard how he yells. But that's not it. I—I can handle him. My father just reminded me that it's my life. Grampa can be a real problem, but only because I love him. But it's not that. That's really nothing. Because it's tangible. I can touch and fight a problem like that."

Luke shook his head. His eyes were still on her, deep, probing, glittering their magical, compelling gold. But again she thought that a guard had slipped over them.

"What is the problem? I love you, Donna."

"Luke—this has all been so fast!" Donna said and, she added silently to herself, There is still something that you aren't telling me. Was she imagining it? Was there really something mysterious about him? If she loved him, she had to trust him.

"Donna, I love you. And I want you so badly that I'm half insane, tempted to ravage you in the middle of the street. I have to keep reminding myself that I am a priest and am not supposed to do things like that."

She laughed, but she lowered her eyes and slipped an arm through his. She shared the feeling, the hunger, the need. Each time she touched him, thought of him, felt him near, it was there: an electricity, static, tangible, almost overwhelming. So strong she thought she would perish if she couldn't soon ease her desire.

"We need to get the bread," she said, trying to draw him along.

He pulled her back, spinning her around to face him. "I want an answer, Donna."

He could have made a very decent living as a hypnotist, she thought a little resentfully. Had she wanted, she couldn't have fought his hold on her, nor could she draw her eyes from his. She parted her lips to speak. He kissed them again, very thoroughly, until she was breathless. He lifted his lips from hers just barely. He spoke in a whisper that demanded an answer.

"Now, Donna."

Night had fallen, she noted vaguely. They were surrounded by nothing but darkness. Somewhere a dog was barking. Down the street, a lamp came on. But they stood in a shadow. The glint in his eyes was made satanic by the filtering of artificial light.

"Yes," she murmured.

"When?"

"When what?"

"The wedding, Donna. When can we be married?"

"Not until we get the bread."

"Donna!"

"I . . . uh . . . don't know. Is there anything special that you have to do? I've never married a priest before."

He smiled, releasing her and taking her hand. He kissed her fingers idly, touching the tips lightly with his tongue, sucking on them lightly in a manner so sensual she felt her knees weaken and a flash of intense heat fill her body and soul.

"Nothing too special." He smiled and took her hand in his. "Where do we go for the bread?"

"Uh . . . down to the corner," Donna stammered.

His beguilement of her senses was pathetic and sinful. But he had extracted the promise he wanted from her. He began to walk, holding her hand as if they were teenagers, and as they bought a number of Mr. Scrathatelli's fresh Italian loaves, they planned a wedding.

It would take place in two weeks, in New York, at St.

Philip's. He apologized to her for forcing that issue, but it would be in poor taste not to be married in his own church. Father Jaime would marry them. Both wanted to keep the service small, but Donna's family would be invited, and wherever her family went, there was an instant crowd.

It was when they were walking back to the house that Donna suddenly hesitated. "I guess I'll talk to my grandfather tonight," she said.

He laughed. "I don't think it will be so bad. I did my very best with him." He grimaced. "Donna, I hate anisette. I haven't prayed so hard in a long time as I did to manage to imbibe half that bottle with the old man!"

Donna chuckled, but the sound was still uneasy.

Luke sighed. "If you want to do this right, I can talk to your father—"

"We already have father's blessing."

"We do?"

"Yes," Donna said distractedly.

"Then—"

"Oh, Luke, don't you see? I'm twenty-eight years old. I would do what I wanted anyway, but . . ."

"They mean so much to you, right?"

"Yes, is that wrong?"

"No, it's one of the reasons I love you."

She spun around, crushing the bread as she held fast to him. "Is it, Luke? I guess I always wondered a little what you saw. You—you're unique, Luke. But I'm afraid that I'm rather ordinary—"

"Ordinary." He laughed, lifting her clear from the ground to kiss the top of her head. "Stubborn, persistent, determined, caring, and a dozen other things. Ordinary, never. And besides that. . . ."

"What?" Donna demanded.

"I have never, never met a woman with such heavenly, gorgeous, sensual sex appeal."

"Oh!" Donna laughed as she struggled from his arms. "I think you'd better put me down, Father. I think a few members of my family are still thinking of you as a holy man, and I don't want to shock anyone. I think I almost gave my father a stroke tonight."

Luke smiled and set her down. "I'm serious!" Donna charged him indignantly. She walked ahead of him, then suddenly stopped, swinging around again.

"Oh, Luke! We can't be married yet! Not unless Lorna can be there. Luke, she's my best friend—"

"Donna!" His voice grated with a frustrated impatience. "Trust me! Lorna will understand."

Trust me. . . . She was always being told to trust him and she did. Didn't she?

"Donna! It'sa cold outta there! You come up, now!"

She gazed up at the old triple decker. Her grandmother's head was sticking out of the window. "Coming!" she called back.

She grimaced at Luke. "Are you sure you know what you're getting into?"

"I'll love every minute of it," he promised her dryly. "Except once we're legally married, I think I am going to have to tell your grandfather that I hate anisette."

Donna hurried up the walk with him close behind her. He caught her in the stairwell and spun her around for one last quick kiss.

"Donna, two weeks."

"I just wish—"

"Have mercy! I warned you that I wasn't a saint."

She nodded, swallowing quickly. Then she hurried on up the rest of the stairs.

Dinner was delicious. Luke met more of her aunts, uncles, and cousins. He seemed at total ease with the cacophony, and she was grateful for his understanding that as chaotic as it all was, her family was special.

When she walked him to the door to leave, he told her firmly that he would wait downstairs. She gave up trying to dissuade him and returned to the kitchen. She met her father's eyes, and he smiled his encouragement to her.

Her grandfather was sitting at the butcher block table again, still impeccably neat in his white shirt and suspenders. He was playing a game of solitaire and sipping espresso. He didn't look up when she approached, but kept turning his cards over.

Donna realized that the kitchen had gone silent. She wished that someone would make some noise but it seemed as if she was going to have a full and uniquely quiet audience for her confrontation.

Without looking up, her grandfather began to speak. "He's a nice boy, Donna. But he isn't for you."

Donna took a deep breath and squared her shoulders. She knew that things had been going way too smoothly. "I'm going to marry him, Grandpa."

His cards slapped down hard on the table and he stared at her, his jaw firmly squared. "He's not for you! Donna, I—your grandpa—am telling you no!"

Donna started as someone touched her shoulders. Her father was standing behind her. "Pop, Donna is old enough to do as she pleases. She's been wise enough to choose a good man. Give her your blessing."

Donna's grandfather swallowed down his espresso and picked up his playing cards as if no one had spoken.

"Pop, Donna is my daughter, and I'm going to be proud to give her to such a man."

"I will not be there."

"That will be your choice."

Donna closed her eyes for a brief moment, gathering strength. She wasn't going to have her father and grandfather fighting because of her. She gave her father a brief smile and went to kneel by her grandfather. He kept playing cards. Donna waited.

At last he looked up; his blue eyes rheumy with age caught hers; they were rebellious and pained, and Donna thought of how he had always grumbled and chastised them—and how he had also always been there to soothe away all the little hurts that were a part of growing up.

"Grandpa," she said quietly, "I think you know that I love you and I would never want to hurt you in any way. But I love Luke Trudeau, and I am going to marry him. It will hurt me deeply if you don't accept him, but whether you do or not, I am going to marry him. Whatever he is, Grandpa, he's a good man first. And I want him because he is a good man."

Stony silence followed her speech. Then she was treated to a burst of angry Italian she couldn't begin to follow though she had been hearing it all her life.

"Grandpa—"

An old and boney finger wagged threateningly at her. "I won't be at your wedding, Donna, you hear me—I won't be there!"

"I'll miss you, Grandpa."

Donna rose, kissed his forehead, and headed for the door. She had known this would come, she had known, and yet it hurt so badly, because she did love her grandfather. Walking away from him was one of the hardest things she had ever done.

"Donna! Don't you walk out that door!"

"Pop—" her father interrupted.

"I'm not talking to you, Sal! Donna, I'll come to your wedding. But don't ask me to dance!"

Donna froze where she stood for a minute. Then his words sank into her mind with sweet clarity. Thank God! Oh yes, thank God—maybe He was intervening!

She spun around, racing back to his chair and kissing his balding head. "Thank you, Grandpa!"

She hugged him until he cried out that she was going to crush his bones. Then she whirled about and kissed everyone in the room, which took her a little while.

She kissed her mother last, then raced down the stairs. Luke was leaning against his rented car, smoking a cigarette. She hurled herself into his arms. "Oh, Luke, it went perfectly—well, almost perfectly."

"Did it?" he asked her huskily. "Then let me take you home in perfect shape. When you're this enthusiastic, it's very hard to convince myself you'll be morally and legally mine very soon. . . ."

Perfect. Yes, it would all be perfect.

If only things would straighten out for Lorna, and if only she understood this man shrouded in mystery.

CHAPTER ELEVEN

Luke returned to New York the next morning without seeing her again. Once he left, Donna began to doubt her sanity. It was crazy. Absolutely crazy. She was marrying a man she barely knew. She had made promises, forgetting all about her own life.

Everything suddenly became a crisis for Donna—her house, her job, everything.

But everything was solved too easily. Her oldest brother wanted to buy her house, and since she did the bookkeeping for the business, her father saw no reason why she couldn't continue handling the business accounts from New York.

She had called Luke. Did a priest's wife do such things? His laugh had touched her with warmth and a flood of anticipation. Sure, whatever she wanted to do was fine with him.

In just two weeks she would be married. It should have been an awful rush, impossible to accomplish. But her sisters packed her belongings, her brothers worried about settling her accounts, and she was left with very little to do.

Perfect.

Luke called again to tell her that he had arranged for her family's priest to preside along with Father Jaime at the ceremony.

Again she was touched by his consideration and by the sound of his voice. She knew that her family would be thrilled.

Perfect.

Perfect again.

Then why was she so nervous . . . so unsure? She loved him, she needed him. Despite the nagging feeling that something was being withheld from her, she knew she would ten times rather worry with him than to have to live without him.

And so the days sped quickly by.

On the Friday before the wedding, a wing of suites at the Plaza was taken over by the Miro family. Dina—a bundle of energy for a change—worked studiously to move Donna's things into Luke's house. Her suitcase, packed for a honeymoon "in a warm clime," was left at the foot of Luke's bed. There was a dinner party at which Donna met Luke's family. (Not as large as her own, but she was already dreading Christmas shopping!) His sisters were charming, his father a handsome doll, and his mother as sweet as could be. She had been thrilled to meet Donna.

Perfect. Everything was perfect.

Except that Andrew wasn't there, nor was Lorna. When asked about his brother, Luke just said that he was away on business, and, unfortunately, just couldn't make it back.

At ten o'clock, the families dispersed and Donna was left alone with Luke. Suddenly she felt how very deeply she *didn't* know him. Shivers raced along her spine, tremors of foreboding. Now, she told herself. Now was the time.

Her throat seemed to constrict, and she felt at a loss. How did she put it into words? How did she ask him what it was he was hiding from her, why he never talked about April? Ask, she told herself. Open your mouth and ask. . . .

But then he was walking toward her with his long strides, filled with a leashed tension. She felt that gold and sun touch of his eyes, and her shivers became a cascade of heat when his arms came around her. His lips touched hers, then his hands, large and tender, holding, cupping, exploring. Firm, knowing . . . then gossamer light . . . making her ache. . . .

"I'm going to take you back to the hotel," he told her.

It was raining, and cold. Not even Luke could manage to get a cab quickly. They stood on the steps, huddled beneath the overhang as they waited.

It was a dreary night, promising little better for the morrow.

"Luke?" Donna finally asked.

"What?"

"Why don't you ever talk about April?"

She felt him tighten. "Because she's dead."

"I know, but . . . Mary said once that you had loved her very much."

126

"Of course I loved her. Very much. But she's dead, and there's nothing I nor anyone else can do about it now."

His tone was blunt. Curt to the point of annoyance. Rudeness.

"Luke! I feel that you're hiding something from me—"

"For heaven sake, Donna! What do you want me to say? That it hurt? Yes, it hurt badly. No, I'll never forget it or her. That's natural. But it's not something to harp on. I don't hide anything from you. Not that you need to know."

"That I need to know?" Donna echoed. She heard the sound of the constant drizzle of the rain. It seemed to tear at her and ridiculously beckon her to cry along with it. She felt terribly cold, terribly wet, suddenly frighteningly alone.

"Luke," she said stiffly. "You say that you love me. We're getting married tomorrow. It isn't that I need to know things, it's just that—"

"There's the taxi! Hurry, or we'll get drenched."

She felt herself propelled down to the sidewalk and into the cab. Luke asked for the Plaza, then settled back beside her.

The neon lights were casting strange glints on his eyes again. He looked satanishly handsome—the dark hypnotist again. Except that he wasn't looking at her, he was staring into the night.

"Luke," she began, but before she could say more, he had twisted and taken her into his arms. His whisper was for her alone.

"Donna . . . please, let it lie. I have you. I love you. It's all I ask from life."

The doubt was gone. The fear was gone.

One more day and she would be his wife. . . .

Morning dawned with the same drizzle. By midafternoon it was still dark and gray. Night would come quickly.

Donna wasn't really bothered by the weather. She hadn't wanted a big, ostentatious wedding; she'd already had one, and not even an annulment could change that. She and Luke had both been married before, so their five-o'clock wedding was planned to be a simple one.

She wore pale-blue silk and carried a handful of baby's breath. A Catholic and an Episcopalian priest would conduct the ceremony and mass. Luke—and Donna's grandfather—had made all the arrangements.

The church was full. She should have expected it. Her family alone could fill a quarter of the pews.

But it seemed that word had gone out among Luke's parishioners, and not one of them wanted to miss his wedding. She smiled a little, knowing Luke would never turn anyone away.

A flute played as she walked down the aisle on her father's arm.

But it was then that the shivers began again. It was almost a case of panic. But that was natural, wasn't it? Weren't all brides and grooms supposed to have shivers, last-minute nerves?

She couldn't call it off now. She couldn't. A church full of people were staring at her. Smiling. Her mother and grandmother were crying, of course, whispering to each other, and Luke . . . was waiting.

A dozen things flew through her mind. She wanted to stop, to make time stand still. No, she couldn't call it off. She pulled dozens of people into the city, not to mention a Worcester priest. They would all kill her.

But if it was wrong, it would be better to stop now. Now, before she became his wife. . . .

Her father placed her hand into Luke's. It was warm and strong and reassuring. She inhaled the scent of his cologne, she felt the power and tension emanating from his tall, darkly handsome form. Again his eyes touched hers. Gold fire, fascinating fire. A blaze of warmth that seemed to promise it was all right. . . .

Of course, when they asked her to say "I do" she could always say, "I think so, but would you all mind waiting for just a minute? I just need the answers to a riddle I don't understand. Doesn't this man seem a little secretive to you? Luke, what is it that you don't want me to know?"

"I do." Luke had spoken. Clear, sure. His husky tenor drifting to her, encompassing her, seeming to caress her.

"I do." She had spoken. And now she was his wife.

No more thinking about it. No more worrying. It was done, for better or worse, until death . . .

Death. April had died. April, whom he wouldn't talk about. "Donna . . ."

She felt his kiss. Slow . . . and then quick. Proper . . . and yet a yearning promise of the night to come. . . .

128

Then suddenly everyone was cheering. Cheering? People didn't cheer at weddings, but she reminded herself this was Luke's wedding.

They had barely made it down the aisle before people were grabbing her, hugging her, kissing her, wishing her the very best for the future.

Donna felt a little lost. Luke had been pulled away from her. There was to be a small reception in the hall behind the offices. Small! she thought with a little panic. There were at least two hundred people there.

"Hey, wife!"

His whisper warmed her ear. She felt his hands on her shoulders, his length behind her as he leaned low. She tilted her chin to catch his grin and quick reassurance.

"In just a few hours we can be on our way."

She smiled. As long as he was near her, she felt warm, felt the certainty that she could have never lived without him once her life had crossed paths with his.

"Have you met the ladies in the bridge club?" he asked her, suddenly flashing a white smile.

She spun about. A horde of matrons was descending on them. She felt like kicking him, and then she felt like laughing. "No, I haven't met the ladies of the bridge club yet."

"Be charming, will you?"

"No problem, Father."

She was charming and she was charmed. The group was wonderful, welcoming, thrilled to meet her, and so very happy for her and for Luke.

"We're just ever so glad!" exclaimed one little woman with a beautiful shade of neatly groomed silver hair. "April's death was such a tragedy! And Luke is such a handsome, vital man. Half the women are in love with him—the young ones and the old ones too!" She laughed. "We didn't think he'd ever marry again. But now, Luke has you! And you're just lovely, dear."

"Thank you so much," Donna murmured. Why did the conversation bother her? April Trudeau's death had been a tragedy. She had been very young, and very beautiful.

They moved into the hall, and Donna sipped champagne, received more good wishes, and was exceedingly grateful that her family was Italian and that her mother and grandmother

129

had been in charge of the food. There was enough to feed an army.

She was grateful once again when Luke's mother caught her arm, excused them both sweetly, and hurried her out the rear door of the hall. "Can you get back to the house by yourself, Donna? You need to grab your things and be ready to go. Luke ran into one of the choir rooms to change."

"Yes, yes, I can find the house!" Donna said.

Luke's mother smiled at her, squeezing her hands. She looked as if she were about to cry, but she hugged Donna. "I hardly know you, dear, but I feel that we'll be great friends."

"I think so too," Donna answered, returning the hug. I hardly know your son, she thought. But . . .

"Have a wonderful time. You'll come to dinner as soon as you get back?"

"Of course!"

"Oh . . . you'd better hurry! It's so gray it's hard to tell when it's raining and when it isn't. Run along!"

With a last quick hug, Donna did, making a mental note to make Luke's family a first priority when they came back from their honeymoon and settled down to normalcy.

Just as she reached the house, the heavens seemed to let loose. Donna thrashed quickly through her bag for the double key set Luke had given her last night. She slammed the door behind her and fumbled for the light switch in the hallway. Brightness vanished the gray, and she paused for a minute, a little awed, a little thrilled—a little disbelieving. She had really married Luke. She was his wife, this was her home. And Luke . . . Luke was hers. . . .

Not if she didn't get her things together and be ready, she thought dryly. The unexpected size of the wedding had surely thrown off their timing. She wanted to be ready to run out the door the minute he appeared.

Donna hurried into his bedroom. She didn't allow herself idle time to fantasize about her future in the room; she pulled out her suitcase, decided on a lightweight suit, shivering as she did so. It felt so cold but she was honeymooning somewhere warm, and she didn't want to get off the airplane and find that she was wilting. Not on her wedding night. . . .

She paused suddenly, holding perfectly still and frowning.

130

There had been something . . . some sound from the office. Little fingers of dread tripped along the small of her back, and she listened intently. Nothing. . . . But then she heard it again. The sound of the window.

It crossed her mind that she should tell Luke the front door didn't need a double lock when entry through the windows seemed to be so easy. But then she forgot about witty comments she might make later, because she was suddenly positive someone was in his office.

Cautiously and silently, she grabbed her purse and crept down the hall, trying to convince herself that the intruder was only Andrew, hoping to catch one of them.

But what if it wasn't Andrew? She needed to run now and find out later. But she couldn't get to the door to run—not unless she went past the office.

Tiptoeing and barely breathing, she paused at the office door. She swallowed hard and edged just close enough to see inside.

It wasn't Andrew. There was a woman quietly lowering the window. Donna's brow furrowed with puzzlement. She had seen the woman, briefly, before. She had been standing in the back of the church during the service. She wore a low-brimmed hat, gray-tinted glasses, and a trenchcoat with the collar pulled up high. Against the cold and the rain, or because she was hiding something?

She was tall and slender, blond—and drenched as badly as a drowned rat. Go now, Donna warned herself, run, and find Luke. . . .

But she didn't run. She stared open-mouthed as the woman turned around and let out a panicked scream as she realized that a shadow was watching her.

It was Lorna who ran, hopping back out the window in a wild panic.

Donna tried to call her name to reassure her, but her first cry came out as a whisper, and Lorna was out of the window before she could yell again. "Lorna!" Damn! Lorna hadn't seen her, only a vague form in the hallway. "Lorna! Wait! It's me, Donna!"

Barely pausing for thought, Donna raced for the window and crawled through it. She could see her friend running down the street, trying to hail a taxi. Donna paused, then streaked after her, barely aware that she was destroying her blue silk. "Lorna!"

The figure continued to run. Donna stopped in dismay as she saw a taxi halt and Lorna hop in. "Lorna!" She screamed again. The taxi started to move as Donna kept running. She would never get another cab, not in the rain.

But she began to believe in miracles when she saw another taxi pulling to the corner. The driver pushed open the door and, with no hesitation, Donna hopped in.

"Where to, lady?"

It didn't strike her just how ridiculous she would sound until she spoke. "Ah . . . just follow that cab, please."

"Which cab?" There were cabs all over the place.

"That cab!" She pointed out the Checker that Lorna had taken. It was over a block ahead of them.

"It's your fare, lady, but if you ask me, you've been watching too much television."

"Just follow the cab, please," Donna said with the best effort at dignity she could muster.

Maybe the cabbie had been watching too much television himself, because he did try. He tried so hard that Donna felt as if her heart was lodged in her throat for the entire ride. But somewhere—where, she didn't know—they lost sight of the Checker.

"What now, lady?" The driver asked her.

But before she could answer, Donna spotted the cab. It was stopped at the corner, half hidden by a produce truck. Lorna was nimbly climbing from it.

"I'll get out!" Donna replied. She scrambled in her purse for the cab fare and paid him, yelling out that he should keep the change.

Apparently it was more than an ample amount. "Thanks, lady!" he yelled to her. "You keep watching that television of yours, you hear?"

Donna barely heard him as she dashed down the street, trying to thread her way through an incredible number of people for such a stormy night. When she reached the corner, there was no sign of Lorna.

Refusing to accept defeat, Donna walked along the block of shops. Lorna couldn't have disappeared into any of them; they were all closed. Donna kept walking anyway, until she was ready to cry.

The rain came again. Only when she started to shiver in earnest did it suddenly occur to her that she hadn't the faintest idea of where she was.

And then she paused in horror. Luke! Oh, no, he had to be wondering what happened to her. She should have been ready for her honeymoon twenty minutes ago!

He would understand. Surely he would understand, she thought frantically.

Are you crazy? she asked herself. He wasn't going to understand how she chased after Lorna in the pouring rain like an idiot.

Donna started searching the streets for a cab. And now—now when she needed it so desperately!—the cabs that rushed by, sending puddles of cold rain splashing over those who tried to hail them, were all full.

She had to get to a phone. She started looking and when she found one, discovered that the receiver had been torn out. She glanced around uneasily and finally realized that she hadn't ended up in the best part in town.

Whistling against the darkness and the rain and the people—who all looked sinister now—Donna started walking again. She found another phone, one with a receiver. But when she started to tear her purse apart, she hadn't a single coin.

She stood on the sidewalk, cursing her own stupidity, until a form rose from the shadows and approached her. "Hiya, honey," the drunk muttered.

"Oh, go straighten up, will you!" Donna snapped, but she began to hurry down the street in the opposite direction.

Then a small miracle occurred. She heard the sound of wheels driving up beside her and she turned quickly, nervously. It was her original cab driver.

"Lady," he called out to her, "are you in some kind of trouble?"

"Yes, I think I am! But where did you come from? How—"

"I've been tagging you. I'm not the last of the great humanitarians or anything, but I thought you might be in trouble."

"Oh, bless you!" Donna stumbled back into the cab, still

babbling. "Oh, bless you, bless you! And my husband's a priest, so it really should mean something."

He already thought she was crazy. It didn't seem to matter much if he thought her an idiot too.

But he didn't comment until they reached the house. It was dark. Where was Luke? she wondered anxiously.

"Doesn't look like anybody's home," the cabbie commented. "Should I take ya somewhere else?"

"No, no," Donna answered, overpaying him atrociously again.

"My name is Dave Gimbal, lady. Give me a call at the shop anytime, okay?"

"Yeah, thanks," Donna murmured. She stepped from the cab and started rummaging through her bag for her keys. Then she remembered that she had set them on the dresser when she changed her shoes.

"What did I do to deserve this?" She groaned, staring up at the dark heavens.

With a sigh of resignation she turned toward the garden, tripped through the damp foliage, jerked up the window, and crawled over the windowsill.

She had been wrong. The house wasn't completely dark. The desk lamp was burning and the house wasn't empty. Luke, clad in a pair of jeans and work shirt, was sitting on the edge of his desk, the phone in his hand.

She tried to smile against his thundering scowl but it didn't work.

"Donna, where have you been?"

"Lorna was here. I—I tried to chase her."

"Lorna?" Disbelief was written all over his face.

"I swear it, Luke. I startled her, and she ran. And I—I tried to catch up with her."

His eyes raked over her from head to toe. "Just how far did you run?"

"I . . . until I tried to follow her cab."

"In another cab, I presume? Oh, never mind!" he snapped with fury. He pushed the button on the phone and started dialing a number, never taking the searing fury of his stare from her. "Andrew, she's here. You can call off the search. What?" A

134

long pause. "Well, at least she's back too." Another pause. "Tonight I have to agree with you. A pair of idiots!"

Donna stiffened at the tone of his voice. Anger raged inside her, but enough to stop her from shivering from the cold rain.

Luke hung up the phone and crossed his arms over his chest. His casual stance was deceptive, but she knew him better. He was about as casual as a cobra about to strike.

Her shivering increased as she remembered the night that they had met, the way he had plucked off the young mugger with a grip that could crush bone.

"You could have both gotten yourselves killed!" Luke snapped so suddenly that his voice was like a whipcrack in the room. Donna forced herself not to jump.

"Luke, you have to understand that it was *Lorna*—"

"Yes, it was Lorna. And between the two of you, you had half the police in New York running wild goose chases in the rain."

"But why . . . ?"

Luke stood. He began talking slow, menacing steps toward her. "Why? Lorna just had to make an appearance at your wedding. She slipped past her guards, intending to slip back— just to be at your wedding. *Wedding*, Donna. Remember?"

"Yes, yes, of course I remember," Donna said, inadvertently backing away from him. "It's just that when I saw her, and when she ran—"

Her voice died away as he kept approaching. For the first time she really noticed the difference in their heights. And for the first time she was really frightened of him. She could see a pulse ticking furiously at the base of his throat, the ripple of muscle as he moved with athletic agility . . . slowly . . . like a tiger about to come in for the kill.

"Luke . . ." She murmured, panic setting in as she skirted around him, trying to put the width of the desk between them. "Remember, you're a priest." She tried a smile and a weak play at humor. "Priests aren't supposed to go crazy and beat their wives. Oh! Luke . . . please!"

In a swift movement, he had hoisted himself over the desk to capture her wrists and pull her hard against him.

"I'm not going to beat you!" he said heatedly, his arms sliding around her. "Although I'd like to shake you until I could

135

rattle some sense into that impulsive head of yours! Don't you realize there's a killer looking for Lorna? You might have led him to her, or gotten . . . oh, God! Don't ever do something like that to me again!"

She was not the only one shaking, Donna realized as her hand had instinctively come to his chest, and she felt the quiver of muscle in that hardness. "Luke," she murmured, "I'm sorry, really sorry. But she ran! Why did she run?"

She couldn't see his eyes, she was being held too tightly against him. "Either she thought you were one of Simson's men, or Andrew."

"Andrew!"

"Umm. He would probably skin her alive. *Is* possibly skinning her alive—"

"Why . . . ?"

"Shut up, Donna."

"What . . . ?"

He pushed her away to stare at her, his eyes intensely gold and narrowed with anger again. "The honeymoon is over. We've missed our plane, and there isn't another one until tomorrow."

"Luke, I'm sorry, I really am. But you have to realize. . . ." Donna paused. He didn't look as if he realized anything. She turned away, pretending to saunter calmly toward the fire and warm herself by its low flame. "I do know how serious the situation is, and she means so much to me. You have to understand—"

She broke off, spinning back around, when she heard his footsteps coming toward her again. Not a slow stalk. A hurried, swift and angry pace. She saw his features, taut and grim.

"Luke!" she cried out, her eyes widening with alarm as she held out a hand in self-defense. "Luke, please, calm down. Let's be rational here—"

Her gesture was useless, her hand was swept aside. She felt his fingers on her, undoing the sodden buttons of the blue silk. "Donna! I am rational! I wish you'd quit trying to talk! I have done—and will always do—anything that I can to help Lorna. But damn it, Donna, I don't want to hear anything more about her tonight!"

His fingers worked quickly. The sodden blue silk fell to the floor. He stood back a second, staring at her in her slip and the low-cut lacy bra. She saw something in his eyes change. Gold to burning amber. His hand came to her, his forefinger, lightly stroking over her cheek, his knuckles, falling to brush over the mounds of her breasts. Donna began to tremble all over again.

"Today," he told her huskily, "we were married. And I've waited too long for you, Donna. Tonight . . . is ours."

She nodded, feeling the trembling deep within her. She shivered, but in her womb, she was hot. She could barely breathe. She had wondered and wanted so long too. And now, now she was his wife. She could touch him. Have him. Reach out and take all that was him, luxuriate in his physical splendor. . . .

He released the front clasp of her bra, smoothed his hands over her flesh, and edged the straps from her shoulders. She heard his intake of breath, felt his eyes as their hungered gaze raked her breasts. She was suddenly shy, suddenly longing to crawl against him and escape that gaze that made her feel as if she burned . . . and ached . . . and longed for more.

But she didn't move, as his hands moved to her waist, then upward, until he cradled her breasts, cupped them, as if he tested their firm weight and found them to be perfect. His palms grazed over the nipples, and they hardened into twin peaks as a low moan escaped from her throat. She tore her eyes from his as she leaned heavily against him.

He slid down her body until he knelt at her feet. Her fingers braced into his shoulders as he removed her sodden shoes one by one and tossed them across the room. She felt his hands graze over her knee, along her thigh . . . travel to her waist, and then she felt the delicious rasp of silk as her stockings were swept away. He stood then, eyes locked with hers as his palms coursed over her hips, finding the elastic of her last garment, and forced the slip to fall in a soft flutter to the floor at her feet.

He stepped away. She could cling to him no longer. But the touch of his eyes caressed her and held her. She stared at him, loving his look and his hunger and the hot and beautiful way he could make her feel just by savoring the naked sight of her.

He came closer again, not touching her. "I knew you would be beautiful," he whispered to her hoarsely. "But not so . . . perfect. . . ."

His voice touched and teased her earlobe, his breath warmed

and thrilled her. Donna emitted a little cry and threw her arms around him.

"Donna . . ." He murmured, his voice muffled against her hair. "I want you . . . now."

Kisses, light, nipped; the touch of the tip of his tongue, the graze of his teeth, found her throat . . . her earlobes. Her own breath rose on a jagged plane to meet and mingle with his. She continued to cling to the solidity of his shoulders to stand. "Luke . . ." she whispered a soft plea. It was all that she could do.

The fire burned warm in low embers behind them. He stepped back from her again, gazing at her with desire tautening and darkening his features. Donna lifted a hand to him, but he caught it and remained still, savoring her. Shadows and glimmers of golden light were cast over her angles and curves. Her breasts gleamed with that gold, full and firm, over the shadows of her ribs, the trim waist. Her hips were full, rounded, inviting; her legs were long for her height, shapely . . . beautiful . . . gold against the fire. He could stare at her forever. He could never drink in all of her. . . .

He moved toward her, pressed his lips to hers, loved them, revered them. Then his tongue filled her mouth with his hunger, sweet and warm and passionately exciting. Donna returned the kiss, awed at the response he could elicit in her. Nothing mattered when he touched her. No concern or fear could haunt her in his arms.

She stood on tiptoe and pressed her body to his, the softness of her form against the hardness of his. Her fingers played with the hair at his nape that curled over his collar. Roamed his shoulders, his back . . . slipped beneath the waistband of his slacks. The vibration of his groan trembled against her and through her. She slid her fingers around until they met at his buckle. She was as sure as he as she released it. She half laughed and half cried with frustration as his zipper refused to give way to her fingers.

Luke stepped back again, kicking off his loafers. She was certain that she ripped away half the buttons in her haste to remove his shirt. She could wait no longer. She threw herself against him again, luxuriating in the feel of the dark hair on his hard chest, teasing, pressing her breasts. He laughed huskily, and she heard the rasp of his zipper giving. He was gone from her for a moment as he shed the pants and his briefs, and then he was holding her, touching her, taking her lips, her throat, the hollows of her shoulders with kisses of spiraling passion.

Against the soft flesh of her belly, she felt the strength of his desire. Hard and potent and so insinuating that she moaned his name, losing all thought except of her need for him.

She forgot that they stood in his office, that they were newly married, that a plush bed awaited them down the hall. She brought her fingers to his face, cupping his chin in her hands, savoring the rough texture of his cheeks. High on her toes, she kissed him and then slid her body against his. It was her turn to explore, and she did. Touching, kissing, tasting his flesh, utilizing secrets so recently learned from him, charting out patterns over his shoulders with just the moist tip of her tongue. Her fingers threaded through the thick dark hair on his chest, followed that triangle until it narrowed at his waist.

He responded to her every touch, his lean, powerful frame trembling, whispered words of encouragement that increased her own spell of passion and desire. She trailed lower and lower against him, unaware that she had ever been afraid of him, that she had feared for her soul for wanting him with such lust. To love him so was a carnal venture, yet nothing had ever felt so pure or so right, or so utterly delicious and primal.

"Yes . . . yes . . . Donna. Touch me . . . love me. . . ."

The deep rasp of his tone thrilled her. She had never felt such sensations, nor had she known the bounds of her own sensuality. Hesitancy was lost, inhibition fell to the flame of her desire and love. She touched and loved him, knew him, held him, explored, and savored his groans, his hoarse whispers, and the knowledge that she drove him to a fever pitch. She slid to her knees, leaving no part of him unloved, until he buckled down before her, grasping her into his arms and laying her before the fire. He rose over her, his lips touching her forehead . . . her nose . . . her mouth . . . then falling to her breast. She whimpered with the sensation as the hardened peak was drawn into his mouth, bathed with the lash of his tongue, drawn inward once again. His dark head moved lower, his tongue delved into her navel, swept her abdomen.

"Luke. . . ."

She tried to grab his hair. The sensations were becoming so exquisite that she could hardly bear it.

"Do unto others . . ." he whispered huskily.

"Ohhh. . . ."

She didn't feel the hard floor, she felt only his touch and her response. Her body began to move, arching, writhing. His kisses flowed over her, through her, into her while the erotic touch of his hands cupped over and adored her breasts. At last she sobbed out his name, and he hovered over her once again, his eyes catching the flame as they stared into hers. He didn't speak then, he moved purposely, shifting, coming into her, a stroke that united them with a sweet and shuddering force. His body closed over hers like a velvet blanket, moving with it, an undulating power that encaptured her heart and soul and passions in a tumultuous rhythm.

Her lashes lifted slightly. She saw a flicker of burning gold and red. A flame in the fire. Reaching . . . high . . . just as she did. Something beckoned, deliciously elusive, a pinnacle that had to be reached. And then time hung suspended. Sensation filled her like sweet wine. She drifted, quaking, floating, holding on to the moments of fulfillment and awesome beauty.

She stared at him with that same awe as he lifted his head, stroking a damp tendril of hair from her face. He lifted a brow, and she smiled demurely, lowering her lashes.

"Bless you, Father," she murmured chastely.

His laughter filled her. "I'm glad to see you've gotten over the fact that I'm a priest."

Donna looked up at him and innocently ran a finger through the hair on his chest. "I never knew just how 'divine' life could be."

"Didn't you?" he teased, catching her hand, kissing her fingers, swathing them erotically with his tongue.

Her smile faded, her breath caught in her throat. Her eyes met his intently. "No," she whispered seriously.

He released her hand and stood. She marveled at the taut beauty of his body as it was silhouetted by the fire.

She didn't have long to allow her eyes that lazy pleasure. He reached down, sweeping her into his arms. Donna laced her arms around his neck, her eyes locked with his.

"Mrs. Trudeau," he said lightly, "I want to spend the entire night showing you just how divine life can be. But in the bedroom. I'd hate to have you unable to function because of rug burns when we do leave for our honeymoon."

"Can we still go?" Donna cried.

"Umm. We'll just be a day short."

"I'll make it up to you," Donna promised.

"Yes," he said in mock anger. "I intend that you will."

She chuckled as he raised a diabolical brow. But as his long strides carried them down the hallway, she touched his cheek.

"You've known a lot of women, haven't you, Luke?"

He sighed. "I've told you, Donna, I'm not a saint, and I wasn't born a priest. I'm afraid that you're far more the angel than I am. A sensuous angel, at that."

His foot nudged open the bedroom door. Donna felt herself encompassed by the softness of the bed, made warm by the heat of his body.

"I love you, Luke," she whispered.

"Donna . . . I love you. I can't tell you how much . . . ever."

"Show me . . . please."

"What . . . a . . . divine request."

His words were broken as his kisses seared her flesh once again. His hands moved on her, showing her breasts an absolute adoration.

"I've never felt more . . . moral." Donna gasped. "Or"— she breathed to him with an erratic whisper a moment later— "more deliciously . . . wickedly . . .

Excitedly . . .

Delightedly fulfilled and Loved."

CHAPTER TWELVE

Luke sat back in his chair, idly drumming his fingers over the desk rather than the typewriter that sat before him. He was supposed to be writing his Sunday sermon. But it was hard to write a sermon when he'd just returned from his honeymoon.

A week in the sun. Blue skies, bleached sand beaches, an aqua surf. A small cottage with complete privacy . . . Donna. The two of them making love on that bed of damp sand beneath that brilliant sky . . . beneath a benign moon. In the crystal-clear water. . . .

A little tap sounded at his door and he started. "Yes?"

Donna popped her head in, then entered. They had left the heat and clear skies behind them; winter had come with its first snow, which had immediately turned to a grimy slush. Donna was no longer clad in a skimpy bikini, a strapless sundress—or nothing at all. But the sweater she wore molded provocatively to the fullness of her breasts, and being well acquainted with the lush mounds that lurked beneath it, her appearance did little to dispel the sexy thoughts that had come to him with his memory of the island.

"Hi," she said cheerfully. "What are you doing?"

"Writing a sermon," he told her.

She glanced over his shoulder, frowning as she saw the blank piece of paper. "There's nothing written," she told him.

"I know," he said, meeting her eyes with his own gleaming wickedly. "It's hard to write a sermon on today's morals when you can't get your mind off your wife's—" His eyes dropped, level with her breasts. He hesitated, then raised them again, his mouth slanted in a crooked grin. ". . . face."

"That's a problem, isn't it?" Donna teased, crawling onto his lap.

He laughed, playing idly with her hair. "I'm not going to get very far at this rate."

"You weren't getting very far to begin with."

"That's true," Luke murmured, and again his eyes seemed to sizzle into hers. "But if you're going to continue to distract me, lady, I'm going to demand the goods."

She instantly tried to shimmy from his lap but Luke refused to let her go. She dropped her voice to a whisper. "Luke, Mary—"

"Mary never interrupts me when I'm . . . working. We can lock the door."

"Luke—"

She didn't get far with her interruption. He stood quickly, muscles bunching as he carried her with him to slip the lock on the door. "You're crazy!" Donna moaned.

"Hmmm . . ." He murmured, setting her on her feet. His hands slipped beneath the wool of her sweater as his lips settled heatedly over hers. He was crazy, but wonderfully so. He caressed her breast as his lips moved enticingly, his tongue parting her teeth. Donna gave up all thought of resistance and slipped her arms around his neck, meeting his tongue with her own, luxuriating in the shiver of desire that shot through her.

"Ah . . . hemm. Knock, knock."

With a horrified start, Donna broke the kiss, spinning about in Luke's arms. Andrew had just come through the window.

"Andrew!" Luke exploded, a true edge to his voice. "Damn it, Andrew, this has to stop!"

"I know, I know, listen, I'm really sorry, but it's important."

Donna stared at her brother-in-law. As usual, his clothing was less than tasteful—a moth-eaten hat over his unruly hair and an old navy coat. She wanted to throw something at him, but that desire faded as she quickly scanned his features. He looked so tired, strained and tired. Not even his apologetic grin could wipe away his look of exhaustion.

"It's okay, Andrew," she said.

"No, it's not, Donna, but I appreciate your saying so." He gazed from her to his brother. "Luke, I've got to talk to you."

Donna twisted to see her husband's face, waiting tensely. She had read the inference in Andrew's voice, the words left out. I've got to talk to you alone, was what he meant to say.

And what she wanted Luke to say in return was that she was his wife, that he didn't keep secrets from her. That whatever Andrew had to say he could say with her there. . . .

"Donna, will you excuse us."

It wasn't a question at all, not by the tone of his voice. It was a command.

"Didn't you say earlier that you had some accounts to look over for your father?" he continued.

That was point blank. If she were to insist on staying she was certain he would just as politely remove her by force.

She didn't say anything, but stiffened in his arms, then stepped past him, her back ramrod straight as she headed toward the door.

"Oh, Donna!" It was Andrew. She turned to see that he had an envelope raised high in his hand. "I almost forgot."

"From Lorna?" she exclaimed.

"Yes."

She grabbed the envelope, said "thank you" as she left the room and the door open behind her. But before she had traveled halfway down the hall to her bedroom, she heard it click closed and the lock was snapped again.

Her mind was torn between anger at Luke's behavior and excitement over the note. She perched on the bed and tore open the envelope.

Donna,

I heard that I delayed your honeymoon, and I'm ever so sorry! I was just going so stir crazy with all the solitude! I don't think I cared if anything happened to me or not, if I could only get out! And I wanted to see your wedding so badly.

Well, at least I did manage to see the wedding. Please tell Luke that I'm sorry, too. He's a great man, Donna, just what you deserve.

Pity that his brother isn't more like him!

If only I hadn't run! Oh, Donna, all I saw was the lurking shadow. I had no idea it was you. I'm so accustomed to running and hiding. If this doesn't end soon, I will go insane.

Enough about me. I'm trying to tell you how happy I am for you, and I sound like a consumer complaint catalogue instead. Donna, the very best. I'm thrilled, and I can't wait to be invited to dinner!

All my love,
Lorna

Donna pensively refolded the letter, a little smile curving her lips. It sounded just like Lorna to elude a set of guards and steer her own course. "But don't be so reckless!" Donna whispered aloud, as if Lorna could hear her thoughts.

She lay back on the bed, casting an elbow over her eyes as she closed them. It must be horrible for Lorna. The solitude, the waiting. How long could it go on? It had already been months.

She sighed, frowning again as she thought about Lorna's comments regarding Luke and Andrew. Donna had liked Andrew despite everything. She had to assume, if Andrew had been designated Lorna's keeper, that the friction between them rose because of circumstances. Still, she felt more than a little angry with her brother-in-law herself.

But not as furious and frustrated as she felt toward her husband. She was tired of blind trust. Andrew had come because he wanted something, not because he needed the confidentiality of a confession!

"Oh, there you are."

Donna started, swinging up as Luke spoke to her, leaning against the door frame.

"What was that all about?" she demanded.

"Oh, nothing important. Listen, I've got to go out for a few minutes. If you're hungry, go ahead and eat without me. I won't be real late, though."

"Out?" Donna frowned as she quizzed him. "I thought that you had to finish your sermon tonight."

"I have to go out. I didn't come in for your permission. I wanted a wife, not a warden. I just told you, I won't be late."

Stunned, she stared after his back as he turned away from her. She heard his footsteps echo as he moved down the hall.

So much for a marriage made in heaven, she thought bitterly, belatedly reminding herself that she had always known she didn't really understand many things about him. But he had practically slapped her in the face with his words!

She sprang from the bed, coldly determined to find out what was going on. She wasn't a warden, and she hadn't been acting like one. She was his wife, and although she knew realistically that their lives couldn't be a continual honeymoon, she wasn't going to be rudely shunted aside for asking a concerned question!

Donna heard Luke call something to Mary, then the front door closed.

Impetuously she grabbed her coat and purse and raced after him. "Be back soon, Mary!" she called out, exiting and closing the front door as quickly as Luke, determined not to lose sight of her husband.

She hadn't. He was walking toward the corner, hailing a cab. A feeling of déjà-vu assailed her. She had done this all very recently—put herself into a perilous position and caused a rash of trouble.

She paused; she had no right to be following him but she loved him, and she couldn't stand sensing that there was something she didn't know about him.

Donna hurried down the street, glad that at least it wasn't raining. A cab approached and she hailed it.

A feeling of déjà-vu assailed her again when the cabbie asked her destination and she told him to follow the cab ahead. He emitted a sardonic sigh as he took off.

Luke's cab wasn't hard to follow. It led a fairly straight course, zigzagging only at the end of its journey, arriving at the police station.

Puzzled, Donna watched her husband as he walked up the steps and entered the door.

"Seven fifty," the cabbie told her.

Donna paid him and exited the cab, uncertain of what to do next. She wanted to follow him in but she didn't want him to see her.

She entered the chaotic station house. There was no sight of Luke.

"Can I help you?"

She glanced up at a young man in uniform. "I . . . uh, no," Donna stammered. "I was just looking for a friend."

"Maybe she's already been booked," the officer offered helpfully.

"Booked?"

"Maybe she's already in jail," he exclaimed patiently. "What's her name, I'll find out for you."

"Ah, no, no, thank you! She didn't do anything," Donna fabricated quickly. "She had . . . uh . . . just asked me to meet her here because she's doing a thesis. On police work in New York City, you know." Donna flashed him a radiant smile and backed toward the door. "I'll just wait a moment or two longer, if it's okay."

"Certainly," the officer told her politely.

Donna smiled again. He turned away, and she noticed a row of public telephones and hurried to them. She picked up a receiver, glanced around guiltily, and pretended to talk, hoping the phone she had chosen didn't choose to ring.

She began to feel absurd, as if she were on a ridiculous goose chase.

But then she saw him, pausing with what she assumed to be two plainclothesmen to say something to the desk sergeant.

Donna huddled as far as she could into her phone booth, holding her breath in the hope that he wouldn't see her. Luke and the other two men walked right past her.

"Where do you want to start, Luke?" one of the men asked.

Luke hesitated, and Donna noticed that he looked a lot like Andrew had, strained, worn, and very tired. He had just come back from their honeymoon. Why did he look so tense?

"North, I think," Luke replied.

"I'll do the driving," the other man said.

And then Luke was saying something else, but they had gone on past her, and she couldn't hear what he was saying.

Where were they going? Why did Luke look so exhausted?

She should go home. She should trust him. When he was ready to talk to her, he would.

No, she thought, feeling a knot that seemed to constrict about her heart. She had to know what was going on. It was important to her present happiness, to the lifetime that stretched before them.

Without thinking any further, she raced out into the street, quickly scanning the area for her husband. She saw him, near the curb, by a dusty old Chevy. One of the plainclothesmen was climbing into the driver's seat. Luke was getting into the front passenger's seat, and the third man was climbing into the back.

"I need a cab, I need a cab!" she muttered desperately, craning her neck to see beyond the immediate traffic. The Chevy was about to leave the curb. At last Donna saw an empty Checker; she raised her hand and ran for it.

"Please—follow that Chevy!" she told the driver.

"Say, do what now?" the driver inquired. He appeared to be a young Bahamian—nice enough but, like Dave Gimbal, he seemed to think that she was crazy.

"I said follow that Chevy. Listen, sir, I may be a lunatic, but I'm a harmless one, and if you keep that car in sight, I promise to make it worth your while."

"Sure thing," the cabbie said. "It's your money!" He revved his motor, lurching the cab out into traffic.

It was an erratic drive, and finally the Chevy stopped and pulled to a curb.

"What do I do?" the cabbie asked.

"Whatever he does," Donna replied.

The cabbie, remaining a discreet distance back, pulled to the curb. The unmarked police car pulled away.

The cabbie grimaced. "You want me to—"

"Follow it," Donna finished for him.

The cabbie pulled back out into traffic.

Donna grew confused as the police car stopped, then continued several times. The cabbie seemed exasperated, but quietly so. He wasn't about to argue with the fare that was building up.

Finally the police car drew up before an old tenement building. This time when the Chevy parked, the lights went out. "What now?" the cabbie asked.

"I'm not sure yet," Donna whispered. The night seemed conducive to whispering.

A second later Donna saw Luke and one of the plainsclothesmen get out of the car and head toward the tenement.

"Something's happening here, lady," the cabbie said uneasily. "Look."

148

Cars were driving up along the curb all the way down the street—police cars, their lights flashing but their sirens silent.

"Lady," the cabbie said. "I think it's time we get out of here."

Chicken! Donna thought a little scornfully. But then a sigh escaped her. She couldn't blame a stranger for not wanting to risk his livelihood, and the situation didn't look pleasant.

She dug into her bag and paid him, then jerked at the door handle. "Go on, you've been great," she said quietly. "Go ahead and get out of here."

"Wait a minute now, *you* should come with *me.*" This cabbie, it seemed, really was a nice guy too. He was concerned for her.

"I can't," Donna said simply. "I—I have to find out just what is going on."

She stepped out of the cab, noting quickly that the police were beginning to cordon off the street. She would be sent away if she didn't move quickly. A big bush in a small patch of earth in the middle of the cement sidewalk could provide some cover. Moving like a sylph in the darkness, Donna hurried to the bush and squatted low beside it so that the branches would shield her in the darkness.

She heard an explosion that tore at her ears, so sharp that it ricocheted within her head. For a minute she didn't understand; then she realized that between the tenement and the police, volleys of shot were being exchanged.

Luke was in the tenement. . . .

She screamed suddenly as she heard a loud retort and then a softer ripping sound. A bullet had just whizzed through the branches of the bush. Leaves shredded all about Donna, and terror set into her like a blast of arctic wind. She quaked as she fought the urge to faint and the darkness that threatened to consume her.

What was she doing there? she asked herself in belated horror, sinking down as close to the ground as she could. Things seemed to be crawling on her. There were bugs all over the bush. Something brushed her face, and she almost screamed again. What in hell was going on?

Then, suddenly, there was silence. She heard a voice, Luke's voice, shouting from a window high in the tenement.

"We're coming out. We've got Pierce."

Another voice answered him over a bullhorn. "Take him carefully, gentlemen. And make sure someone's read him his rights."

The door to the tenement opened. Donna could see four figures: the two plainclothesmen, Luke, and the man she had to assume to be Pierce.

Donna crawled on the ground. There were lights blazing on the entrance to the house now. The four men were walking down the entryway steps.

Someone suddenly knocked into her from behind. She spun about to see an officer in uniform.

"Lady, what are you doing here?" he demanded in dismay.

"St-standing." Donna muttered out the obvious.

"Well, get out of here!"

"Hey—he's loose and running!" someone suddenly shouted.

"Fire a warning shot!" the voice of authority called out harshly over the bullhorn.

The explosion of a bullet sounded again. Suddenly the officer was shoving Donna, throwing her to the ground. Her head grazed the cement sidewalk, and she was stunned.

"What . . . ?"

She didn't need to ask the question. Heavy footsteps were pounding all about her. The man—Pierce—was trying to escape and the officer had only been trying to shield her from the bullet.

Pierce was racing by her. She saw his legs fly and then she saw him drop to the ground. Someone was grappling with him so close that one good roll would bring the two of them on top of Donna.

The officer was trying to pull her away but that big roll she had been fearing suddenly, abruptly came.

The man who had tackled Pierce was Luke. In the middle of the fight, Luke was suddenly staring into her eyes.

"Donna!" He gasped.

And that's when Pierce hit him—hard, with the wrist that dangled a pair of handcuffs that had never made it around the other wrist.

"Luke!" Donna screamed.

He shook his head; the blow had staggered him. But then he ignored Donna and returned the blow with his own right punch

150

to Pierce's jaw. Pierce was down. A little grunt escaped him, but he fell as sweetly as a kid going to sleep.

But then Luke fell too, right on top of Pierce.

"No!" Donna screamed.

"Come on, lady—let's go!"

It was the uniformed officer again. His grip on her was firm, and he was dragging her away.

"Wait!" she cried, but she could no longer see Luke or Pierce. They were now surrounded by other officers.

Cops were all over the lawn. She was being dragged away and Luke was in the middle of it all.

"Come on along, now, ma'am."

"Wait. I can't. Please! Luke—"

"They'll bring him along in a minute. We want to get you taken care of right away."

"Taken care of—"

She didn't finish. She felt herself lifted, then set down, and she realized she was in the back of a rescue vehicle. Another man in a white coat was easing her shoulders back onto a cot.

"I'm fine!" Donna protested.

The door slammed; the ambulance attendant forced her shoulders down. "Just relax now, we have to see the extent of your injuries."

"I'm not injured!" Donna wailed. "But my husband—don't you understand! I just want to see my husband."

The man spoke in a very practiced, soothing voice. "You're the father's wife?"

"Yes! Yes!"

"He'll be right along. We've got to see to your head injury."

"Head injury?" Donna's fingers came to her forehead. She felt something sticky. Blood. She didn't even remember being scratched. Oh, yes, her head had collided with the sidewalk.

"I promise you, they'll be right along. Now just lie back. . . ."

She could still hear the sirens screaming. Donna gave up and lay back.

She wasn't really injured. She had known she wasn't. She just had a scratch on her head from the brush with the cement, and a few bruises. But they were quick and efficient in the emergency room, and if she hadn't been half out of her mind with concern for Luke, she would have been grateful for the concern shown her.

As it was, she couldn't help badgering the people working over her. And when it seemed that they had finished with their x-rays and bandages, she sat up on the cot and demanded, "I want to know where my husband is now. I want to see him."

An ironclad matron of a nurse gave her a firm smile. "You just sit right here, Mrs. Trudeau. Someone will be with you in a minute."

The nurse closed a white curtain and left her. Donna stared dismally at it. If Luke was hurt, it was her fault. She had been there, she had gotten in the way.

Please God, she prayed quickly, don't let him be hurt. . . .

But, she wailed silently to herself, if he had only trusted her, if he had only been honest with her, she wouldn't have been there.

But that didn't matter. If he was hurt, it would still be her fault. But what had he been doing there?

The curtain moved. Donna glanced sharply at it with high anticipation, getting off the cot quickly. But it wasn't Luke who came through the little opening. It was Andrew.

Donna's outstretched arms fell to her sides. She spun from him in sudden anger, tears glazing her eyes.

"Donna, I need to talk to you."

"Where's Luke?" she asked him bitterly.

"Upstairs."

"Upstairs?" Donna forgot her anger. "What's wrong with him? What happened? How badly was he hurt?" Then suddenly she was running toward him, pummeling her fists against his chest. "I want to know what's going on, Andrew! So help me God, don't tell me to trust you. I want to know what happened."

Andrew caught her wrists, pulled her to him, and tried to soothe her. "Donna, Donna, I came here to try to explain."

She didn't say anything. They could both feel one another's heartbeats.

"Donna, please?" Andrew said quietly.

Anger and strength seemed to seep away from her. She leaned heavily against him.

"You're not going to hit me any more?" he asked, his tone

almost teasing. He wouldn't use such a light tone if Luke were really hurt, she thought, reassured.

"No, I'm not going to hit you any more."

He set her from him, still supporting her. "Get your things. We'll slip into a staff lounge. A little more privacy in case the place should suddenly get crowded."

A few minutes later they were secluded in a doctor's office. Donna sat behind the desk, sipping pale tea in a Styrofoam cup, Andrew was prowling about with a cup of lukewarm coffee.

"Andrew?" she pleaded. "Andrew, come on, I know that you have something to do with this."

"Well, no, actually," he murmured, pausing in his restless pacing to offer her a dry grin. "I didn't have anything to do with tonight at all. It's just that news travels fast in police circles, so I knew what happened, knew that you were here—"

"And Luke?" she implored.

"Luke is okay. Shocking the hospital staff by swearing at them all that he wants to leave."

"I want to see him," Donna said flatly.

"You will," Andrew told her softly. "I just felt that . . . maybe I should give you a few explanations first. I swear to you that Luke is going to be okay. They want to keep him here overnight for observation; he got whacked pretty hard with those cuffs." He paused a moment. "Pierce was a desperate man. He's wanted for five counts of armed robbery in the state of New York; Florida wants him for murder."

A shiver settled over Donna, fear taking hold of her again. God knows what could have happened to her if Luke hadn't been there. . . .

But was this to be her life? What was Luke's connection with the police beyond Andrew?

"You followed Luke, didn't you?" Andrew asked her reproachfully, accusingly.

She lifted her chin. "Yes, I did, Andrew. I had to understand what was going on."

Andrew grinned and at last perched on the edge of the desk. "I told Luke that he should tell you everything. He said you were shying away from him to begin with just because he was a priest; if you knew anything else. . . ."

"Andrew!" Donna placed her cup firmly on the desk. She

was still trembling, but she believed her words were honest. "I love Luke. Nothing changes that, but being kept in the dark makes it very hard."

"My opinion exactly," Andrew said. "Luke was just so scared—"

"Scared!" She felt ridiculously like laughing. She had never thought Luke could be even remotely frightened of anything.

"He fell in love with you. Love is a very powerful weapon."

She looked away. "Go on, Andrew, please."

He sighed. "Okay, I'm just trying to find a place to start." He was silent for a minute.

Donna had to clench her fingers together to keep from prodding him. Then he took so long that Donna decided to prod him anyway. "Andrew, does Luke work for the police?"

"No, I mean, he's not on the city's payroll, or anything. He really is a priest, exactly the man you know."

"So . . ."

"He . . . helps the police," Andrew said at last. "Tonight . . . Donna, Luke gets called in when everyone draws a blank. When the clues don't make any sense. When things get desperate."

Donna shook her head. "I still don't know what you're talking about."

"It's a fifty-fifty shot. Sometimes it works, sometimes it doesn't. But we had a case when you first came to New York. A little girl disappeared. We had nothing to go on. She left school, just as usual, and disappeared. We were stumped. They asked Luke to come in. He went up and sat in her room for a while, and then he was able to tell us that the child's father—the parents were divorced—had taken her. It was true. We found the father, and we found the little girl."

"What are you telling me? That Luke is . . . psychic?"

"I don't call it anything, and neither does Luke. And as I said, sometimes it works, sometimes it doesn't. They've been looking for Pierce for months; he held up a liquor store today, and the bullets went flying. We were lucky a half-dozen people weren't killed. They knew he holed up somewhere afterward; they wanted him fast, before someone else was killed. They called Luke."

Donna stared down at her fingers. They were shaking. What

154

did she feel? Frightened . . . alienated? Yes, she was very frightened. Very unsure. . . .

"There's more to this."

She stared up at Andrew, suddenly certain that she didn't want to hear anymore.

"This Simson thing . . . the case that has us keeping Lorna underground and out of sight."

"Yes?" Her voice sounded thick; too slow.

Andrew sipped at his coffee, as if he had said something that he didn't want to finish. "Do you remember my telling you that . . . one of the first victims died?"

"Yes."

"It was April."

"Oh, my God!" Donna gasped. She felt cold. Numb. And yet through all the coldness, all the numbness, she felt a wrench of pain like a knife wound.

"And it has been one instance," Andrew continued, "where Luke has come up with nothing but blanks."

She felt very, very dizzy, as if she had been caught in a ripping wave from which there was no escape. April . . . the wife he had loved so dearly. Lorna, still caught in a maze of justice, afraid to appear by daylight, losing months and months of her life to the forced necessity of hiding.

And Luke . . . Luke. . . . He hadn't trusted her, he hadn't been completely honest. But she did love him.

The wave seemed to lift from her. The dizziness faded. She stood up, smiling at Andrew.

"I want to see Luke now."

"Maybe you shouldn't. Maybe you should let all this sink in for a while."

"I don't need anything to sink in, Andrew. I'm okay. I'm fine, in fact. Andrew!" she exclaimed in exasperation. "I'm Luke's wife, and I want to see him now."

Andrew smiled slowly, then stood too and opened the door for her with a little bow.

"Room five-oh-two, Donna. If you don't mind, though, I won't join you." He grimaced a bit sheepishly. "My brother isn't fond of other people discussing his business, not even blood relations. I wouldn't want to tempt him to strangle me."

155

She laughed, feeling absurdly lighthearted for all the evening had brought her.

"I thought you had a right to know," Andrew said softly.

"I did," Donna replied. Impulsively she kissed his cheek. "Thank you, Andrew. And Andrew. . . ."

"What?"

"I don't know what's going on with you and Lorna, and maybe that isn't my business. But I'm glad you're in charge. I believe she is as safe as she can be."

"Thanks . . . sis."

Donna smiled. Then she turned to leave him, forgetting all about the one brother in her anxiety to see the other.

CHAPTER THIRTEEN

The light within the room was muted, but she could see Luke clearly. Her lips curled into a small smile; evidently he had eschewed the idea of a hospital gown and won. A stark white sheet was drawn to his chest, contrasting with the gleaming bronze of his body. His hair, too, seemed exceptionally dark against the whiteness of the pillow. The lines of his face seemed exceptionally strong and defined.

Donna moved silently in, quietly sitting in the bedside chair. She started to reach for his hand, stretched on the bed before her. His moved first, enveloping hers.

His eyes didn't open, or maybe the thick black lashes did raise a whisper. "Hi," he said softly.

"Hi, yourself," she murmured, leaving the chair to shift her hips beside his on the bed.

His eyes opened fully. She loved their hazel depths, gold and green, a touch of heaven and of rich, verdant life.

"You've talked to Andrew, haven't you?" he asked her.

Donna started uneasily. "How did you know?"

He closed his eyes, smiling a little bitterly. "No special power of communication, I assure you. I just believe you would have been here before if someone hadn't stopped you. They told me they had released you from emergency half an hour ago."

"Oh," Donna murmured. Then: "Luke, why didn't you tell me?"

He lifted his free hand, then allowed it to fall back to the bed. "I . . . don't know. Maybe I was afraid. I didn't know if you were just so beautiful that I fell in love, or if it was that wonderful streak of sweet and indignant morality that had me so allured. Your concern . . . your absolute determination to find a

157

friend. The more I saw of you, the more I knew that I was right. The chemistry . . . the commitment. Donna, we were unalike in several ways. But very much alike in very important values: marriage . . . loving . . . caring. . . . But·you were so concerned about my being a priest. That was a commitment I had also made for life. I think that I was so worried about surmounting that obstacle in your heart that I was afraid to give you any other reasons to shy away from me."

"Oh, Luke!" Donna, unmindful that she sat in a hospital, leaned low, curving her arms around his neck, blanketing him with her slim body and an abundance of love. His arms in return came around her, holding her tightly.

"I was wrong, Donna," he whispered against her ear. "You had a right to know about April . . . and my work with the police."

Donna planted her hands on his shoulders, meeting his eyes squarely. "Yes, Luke, I had a right to know. And I admit it frightens me. But I don't love you any less." She smiled, smoothing a stray lock of dark hair from his forehead. "And after I became accustomed to the fact that I was in love with a priest, I rather liked the idea."

He raised a brow with a trace of amusement. "Because a priest should make a good husband?"

"Was that wrong?" Donna cross-queried.

He shook his head, enfolding her against his length once again. "No, it wasn't wrong. It just wasn't really relevant. If I were a carpenter, an electrician, or a stockbroker, I would love you just the same. I would want to give, and take, the same things from a marriage. I love you, Donna. So much."

She held tightly to him for a minute, then struggled against the force of his arms, staring down at him again. "Are you really all right?" she asked softly.

His lashes seemed to flicker and fall too easily. "Fine. They just gave me something . . . to relax me."

She chuckled softly. "Probably more to tame you down a bit!" she told him, then the laughter faded from her voice. "I'm so sorry about April, Luke."

His hand squeezed around hers. "I know." He was silent for a minute. "I guess what hurts the worst is that I was so helpless.

I wasn't there . . . but later . . . so many times I've been able to do something. But with this . . . nothing."

She felt the pain in his voice, a haunting anguish. Yet she didn't feel threatened by that first love, only that all that had been given her had been enriched by it. All that she wanted was to ease his sorrow in any way that she could. And all that she could think of to give him was a reinforcement of her own commitment.

"I love you."

A smile flickered over her features, then faded. He reached out and touched her cheek, tenderly grazing it with his knuckles. "I could throttle you for following me tonight," he said gruffly. "If anything would have happened. . . ." He groaned. "It would have been my fault. For not telling you . . . all that you should have known."

"Blind faith, Father Luke," Donna reprimanded him primly. "You have to learn to practice what you preach, my love."

"Maybe I do."

"Talk to me now, Luke," she pleaded softly.

His eyes opened for a minute, touched by the satanish gleam she knew so well. He released her hand to pat the bed. "Curl up beside me, gorgeous, and I'll talk my heart out."

"Luke, this is a hospital—"

"A private room. And besides," he vowed with a trace of solemnity she didn't really trust, "I plan to behave as well as any angel. I just want to feel you near me."

Donna hesitated, then complied, content with the warmth of his body, with the tender power of his arm wrapped around her.

"What do you want to know? I'll do my absolute best to be an open book."

She smiled, unable to resist the temptation to trace his dark brows with her forefinger. "Do I have to watch my thoughts at all times?" she quizzed him, only halfway teasing.

He cast her a withering glance. "Very amusing. I should tell you yes. But that would be a lie."

"I'm sorry, Luke, I shouldn't be joking."

His arm squeezed more tightly about her. He couldn't resist the temptation to give her a slight brush against the full curve beyond her hip.

"Sometimes," he said, his eyes falling closed once again, "we have to joke about important things. Or else we take everything too seriously, and then we're lost. I can't read your mind. I don't have special powers. Nor does God tiptoe into my dreams. To this, I think that science will one day have an answer. The human mind is far more complex than we've begun to know. Sometimes, only sometimes, I can sense things. And if it can help I have to try."

"I know. I'm proud of you."

"Are you really?"

Donna nodded.

She felt his shoulder muscles tense and relax as he shrugged. "I should have trusted you."

She kissed his forehead, his nose, and then his lips, very lightly. "Luke, I knew that I loved you and that was enough. I didn't *need* to know anything more, but because I love you, I want to know you, to understand you completely."

His fingers threaded through her hair, smoothing its length in a tender caress. "You are extremely special, Donna," he murmured. "More precious to me than I will ever be able to tell you."

He held her tightly, and Donna luxuriated in the strength of his love, loath to break away from him. It was a moment she savored; she knew him for all that he was, and she had never felt closer to anyone in her life. Nor had she known it was possible to feel so close, so a part of a man, in body and soul. . . .

"Really, Father!"

Donna started wildly at the voice as a full, glaring light suddenly flooded the room. She jerked from Luke's hold, blinking at the doorway. A stalwart nurse who resembled a Sherman tank was staring at them in horror.

She glanced at Luke. He grimaced. "Relax, Mrs. Simon, this is my wife. Donna"—he gazed into her eyes with another grimace—"meet Mrs. Simon."

"Hello," Donna said with a very radiant and a very false smile.

Mrs. Simon moved into the room, plumping Luke's pillow where Donna had been lying. "It's nice to meet you, Mrs. Trudeau," the nurse said primly, "but this is a hospital, you know."

"Yes, I know," Donna answered meekly.

160

"Please keep that in mind."

"Oh, we will," Luke said. Mrs. Simon muttered a little "hrrmph" and walked to the door. "Donna!" Luke said suddenly in a shocked and husky whisper. "Darling, please! You heard Mrs. Simon. Keep your hands off me!"

Donna stared at him in horror, her jaw falling slack. Mrs. Simon stopped and spun around like a marionette. Donna was beet red, wishing she could smash Luke's pillow over his gleaming eyes.

Luke raised his hands high in the air. "Just kidding, Mrs. Simon."

With her nose lifted high in disapproval, Mrs. Simon stalked out of the room.

"Pull another trick on me like that, Father, and I will have my hands all over you! Tightly—around your neck," Donna threatened.

"Hey, we had to liven up her night somehow. It must get dreary on the late shift."

"She's going to liven me right out of this room," Donna stated dryly. Then she stood suddenly.

"Where are you going?" Luke demanded.

"Home," she told him, "but just for a minute. I want to clean up and grab a few things, then I'll come back. I think that they'll allow me to stay in the chair—if you haven't convinced Mrs. Simon that we're incapable of refraining from lewd and lascivious behavior, that is!"

She thought that he would smile; a frown darkened his features instead. "It's late. I don't like the idea of your running around at night by yourself."

"I'll be perfectly fine, Luke. I'll find a cab home, and I'll take a cab back."

His frown didn't fade. He was obviously having more and more trouble keeping his eyes open, but he caught her wrist, and his grip was strong, far too strong for her to fight.

"Donna, it's too late—"

"Luke, I have to get a few things. My clothes are a mess, my heel is broken and—oh! I won't have to go alone. Andrew is downstairs. I'll get him to come with me."

His hold slowly relaxed. "Okay, but come back quickly."

"I will," she promised, as she brushed a little kiss against his

161

brow. She would, she repeated in a silent vow. She'd never be away from him when she didn't have to be. And if Mrs. Sherman tank had anything to say about it, it would be just too bad, Donna decided firmly.

With that determination in mind, Donna smiled and left the room.

Luke watched her go, still frowning. For some reason, he didn't like it. "Donna!" he called her, but she was gone. And whatever it was that they had given him now caused him to close his eyes.

He gave up and allowed his lids to fall heavily. She was going to be with Andrew. She would be fine. He was just feeling a little spooked because of the night's events. Foolish. Pierce was safely in custody.

A little shudder rippled through him. When he had seen her on the ground, he had never known such fear. But it had ended up okay. Donna was all right, and he was fine or would be, just as soon as morning came and they let him out of his whitewashed, antiseptic world.

His thoughts became incoherent. Donna . . . Andrew . . . Lorna. . . .

Donna knew everything there was to know about him: the dark secrets, the inside things that he had always guarded so closely. And she still loved him. . . . It was a sweet, sweet dream with which to sleep.

Andrew was not downstairs. Distraught, Donna searched the quiet halls, but he was nowhere to be found. The E.R. doctor on duty was not the same man she had seen, and when she described Andrew, the man shook his head blankly and assured her that he hadn't seen him.

Donna hesitated for a minute, certain that Luke would be upset if he learned that she had gone home alone.

Naturally. It had been a traumatic night and it was nice that he was so concerned for her. But it was also a little foolish for him to worry. She could get a taxi, ask it to wait, and come right back. Luke wouldn't even need to know. She was certain that he had fallen asleep as soon as she had left the room.

The desk clerk in the emergency reception area directed her to a phone and she called for a taxi. Congratulating herself on her good sense, she waited within the glass doors of the emergency entrance until she saw the cab pull up.

The driver was a pleasant, talkative man. A native of New York City, streetwise, and interesting as he pointed out buildings of lesser importance in the neon glow of night. Donna feigned polite attention; she hadn't known until she was away from Luke just how much everything was preying on her mind.

She had promised him that nothing mattered; that she loved him. And she meant it. She couldn't imagine life without him now. He was everything good that a woman could want in a man; a rebel in his way, but she knew that his occasional taunts bordering on the irreverent were the lighthearted comments of a very reverent man.

But what was life going to be? They had only just started off on a path that was difficult in the best of situations: marriage. And now . . . she was frightened.

"Is this it?"

"Yes!" Donna exclaimed, getting quickly out of the cab. "Just keep the meter running. I'll be right out."

"Sure thing!"

Donna rushed into the house. Apparently someone had called Mary. She was gone, but the house was as neat as a pin. There was a brief note from her on the dining-room table saying that she hoped everything was fine, and that dinner was in the refrigerator and could be reheated.

Donna grimaced. Once reminded about food, she was starving. But she had a cab waiting, and she was sure she could find something to eat at the hospital, even if it was only junk food from a machine.

She hurried into the bedroom and dug out an overnight bag. She rushed around throwing things into it. Toothbrushes, a razor, Luke's robe, jeans and a shirt, and whatever else struck her as a necessity from the bathroom. With the not so neatly packed bag full, she slammed it shut and rummaged in the closet for fresh clothing. She chose a heavy sweater and a pair of cords, certain that the hospital room would stay cool through the night. She was shivering there, and she knew that hospitals had a tendency to keep the heat low.

Donna gazed longingly at the shower, then reminded herself that she had no time. She undressed quickly and donned the fresh clothing, sitting at the edge of the bed to zip on her boots again.

She frowned, suddenly still and tense. The *zip* sound had seemed to continue after her boot was already secure on her foot.

She held her breath, straining to listen. She could hear the steady tick of the bedside clock, something she never paid any attention to. She could hear the muted sounds of traffic and the quiet within the house. But then it came again. A soft rustling sound, like leaves in the wind—or sheets of paper being rummaged.

Her frown deepened; a shaft of arctic cold raced along her spine. Then she exhaled, the furrows of her frown becoming those of a dry grimace.

The sounds were coming from the study. It had to be Andrew.

She had to be crazy, she told herself as she left the room to walk down the hall. She was married to a psychic priest and had an unkempt undercover cop for a brother-in-law who made all his visit entrances through the windows. But she was happy.

Then it occurred to Donna that it was really an occasion of déjà-vu, and the last time she had heard noises in the study and hurried down the hallway, the nocturnal visitor had been Lorna. Her heart quickened. Was it Lorna? Had something gone wrong? Was she coming to Donna because . . . ? Because of what? If it was Lorna again, Donna didn't want her to run. She felt her breath come in a rush as she neared the door, and without thinking, she began to hurry, heedlessly calling out in a soft tone. "Lorna! It's Donna. Don't—"

She stopped in the doorway. It wasn't Lorna, and it wasn't Andrew. Two men were in the study, dark clad and wearing ski masks. The ridiculous thought hit her that there was no place to ski in Manhattan. Of course not. They were wearing dark ski masks because they were going through Luke's desk.

They were as surprised to see her as she was to see them. But the shock didn't last more than a second. Donna spun about like a whirlwind to run. If she could just reach the front door, she could scream. The taxi driver would be there, and the prowlers would know that an alarm could be radioed in immediately.

The hall had never seemed so long. She was light and agile—and terrified. She could run, and run fast, especially with the strength of the flowing adrenaline.

But just as she reached for the door, her feet were swept from beneath her. The floor rushed up to meet her, hard. A strangled cry tore from her lips, of self-preservation, of pain as the breath was wrenched from her lungs and the impact bruised her flesh. She didn't get a chance to cry out again. A hand clamped over her mouth and she was dragged to her feet. Tears stung her eyes, and she tried to bite. Someone muttered out an oath. A second later the hand was replaced by a dirty scarf.

"I thought you said they were both at the hospital!" one of the men whispered angrily to the other, who was busy binding her hands behind her back.

"They were!" the other snapped back.

Donna kept struggling as she was dragged back into the study.

"Throw her on the sofa, and keep an eye on her!" the first man ordered.

"Why? We might as well get out of here. I've been through the desk. Nothing but bills, sermons, and calendars. If the priest has anything, he ain't got it here."

"I know he's in on it somehow! This is where I followed the girl!"

"Yeah, and it's where you lost her."

Donna landed unceremoniously on the sofa. She lay there stunned, remaining still. She had assumed at first that she had interrupted an ordinary pair of burglars. Ordinary! A moment's faintness gripped her. She breathed deeply, praying that it would pass. Her head cleared. They weren't ordinary burglars, however "ordinary" a burglar could be. They were after Lorna, and they were rifling through the desk and the bookcase again, assuming that Luke had some clue to her whereabouts somewhere.

Suddenly the first one—Red Cap, as she was coming to label him in her mind—stopped, turned around, and stared at her through the eyeholes of the tight ski cap.

"What are you doing?" the second man, Blue Cap, demanded. "We've got to get something, and get out of here."

165

"We've got something," Red Cap said in a deathly tone that seemed to grip Donna's throat and squeeze.

"What are you talking about?"

He pointed a leather-gloved finger toward Donna. "Her."

She knew her eyes widened with fear; her breath seemed to catch, her heart to skip a beat.

"No!" Blue Cap's voice gave her paralyzed heart a moment's flutter of hope. "Listen, I ain't in this for anything big. I was hired to riffle through a house; no one said anything to me about kidnapping."

"Woman-napping," Red Cap corrected. "Hey," he cajoled. "The big man wants the blonde. The blonde came here. I'd say that just might mean that the priest's lovely little wife might know where to find the blonde. What do you say?"

"I'd say that it's kidnapping. That I could be put away for the rest of my youth."

"What youth?" Red Cap taunted. "If we find the blonde for the big guy, we could be worth enough for you to enjoy a few years out at a nice, remote island with lots of wine, women, and song. Think about it."

"It is kidnapping!" Donna tried to shout. All that came out was a muffled plea, which sent Red Cap into gales of laughter.

His laughter cut off abruptly as he turned cold, steely eyes to his companion. "You're in this with me, and I'm taking her."

Before Blue Cap could answer, a thunderous knock sounded at the front door. "Hey, lady!" Donna felt another surge of hope as she heard the cab driver's yell, faint behind the closed door and beyond the long hallway. "Lady! Lady, are you coming? You owe me a fare, you know! If you don't want to pay up, I'll be happy to call the police!"

The surge of hope swelled high within her, as strong as a tidal wave. And it was swept away as quickly as the tide.

"Let's get out of here!" Red Cap snapped. He disappeared but not out the window. He moved to the hallway. Blue Cap stared at Donna uncertainly. But then Red Cap was back, Luke's dark-blue bedspread in his arms.

It was the last thing Donna was to see for some time. Red Cap threw it over her. With as little ceremony, he reached for her, tossed her over his shoulder, and headed for the window.

A few seconds later she was tossed onto something hard. She

heard an engine rev, felt vibrations on the cold flooring beneath
her. Gas fumes caused her to cough. Then she was jolted about
as the vehicle drew into the street.

Luke! she thought with panic and poignancy. He had told her
not to leave him. . . .

CHAPTER FOURTEEN

"Luke!"

He heard his name called, as if from a great distance, or from deep within a dream. Dream. That was it. He had fallen asleep, and he was dreaming.

Still groggy, he half smiled, savoring the sweet, indolent feeling of being half asleep, half awake. Conscious thoughts joined the subconscious. Donna. Maybe it wasn't a dream. She had whispered his name; she was back.

He opened his eyes, stretching and turning, expecting to see her sitting in the bedside chair, watching him with those thick-lashed, sultry blue eyes. The chair was empty; so was the room.

He folded his hands behind his head and stared up at the whitewashed ceiling, wondering why he had awakened when he still felt the physical urge to sleep so strongly.

His eyes closed, flew back opened. He felt instantly, acutely, alertly awake. She should have been back.

Luke rolled over and picked up the bedside phone. He forgot to dial the nine for an outside line, and had to start dialing all over again. His number rang and rang. He hung up and dialed again. One, two, three . . . eight, nine, ten. . . . She wasn't answering.

He hung up the phone, feeling shaky. A cold sweat broke out on his shoulders.

She was on her way back here, he tried to assure himself. She was with Andrew. Maybe they had decided to stop somewhere for a bite to eat. No, Andrew would never risk his cover by appearing with Donna in a public restaurant. Maybe they had ordered sandwiches or pizza somewhere. They were sitting in one of the hospital lounges right now, probably talking about Lorna, hoping that things were going to come to a head soon.

It was no good. He just didn't believe it. He couldn't shake the chills, the cold sweat.

Luke took a deep breath and got out of the bed. A gray fog seemed to swirl around him. He clenched his fists at his sides and drew in another deep breath. Then another. The fog slowly subsided.

The walk from the bed to the closet seemed interminable, but once he reached his clothing and managed to shimmy into his jeans and sweater, he was beginning to feel as if his head had truly cleared and he could walk a straight line. He'd gotten a good bump on his head, he knew, but ironically, it wasn't the bump bothering him now, but the medication.

He checked his pocket instinctively for his wallet and started for the door. Poor timing. Mrs. "Sherman tank" Simon was just on her way in.

"Father Trudeau! Just what do you think you're doing now!"

"Ah, Mrs. Simon! It's been delightful, but I really have to go now."

"Father, you get back in that bed. Do you realize that you're more trouble than a ward full of children?"

"Mrs. Simon, I really am sorry," Luke said regretfully. "I wouldn't make your life *this* miserable if I didn't have to. But I do *have* to leave."

"But you're not dismissed! The doctor has to—"

"Luke! What are you doing?" A new voice interrupted Mrs. Simon. Luke glanced past her to see Andrew standing in the doorway.

"Where's Donna?" he asked his brother tersely.

The confused frown that tensed Andrew's brow was more eloquent than his reply. "She isn't up here with you?"

"No. She left a few hours ago. She said that she was going to run home—with you."

"I haven't seen her since she came up here."

"Something's wrong, Andrew."

Andrew didn't question his brother. He sidestepped Mrs. Simon and hurried to the phone, dialing quickly.

"What *is* going on?" Mrs. Simon demanded.

"You haven't seen my wife, have you?" Luke asked her.

169

"Not since she left, Father, which was the proper thing to do! She did say, though, that she was coming back."

Luke vaguely heard Andrew instructing someone to get to his house. Andrew set down the receiver.

"Father—" Mrs. Simon began.

"Please, Mrs. Simon," Andrew interrupted her. "I'll be out of here in just a few minutes."

"We'll be out of here in just a few minutes," Luke corrected.

"Luke!" Andrew protested. "You can't—"

"I'm the only one who can," Luke persisted.

Mrs. Simon looked from one man to another: a priest who looked like a movie star and acted like a devil; and a long-limbed, unclipped hippy who looked like he'd been dredged out of the nearest sewer.

"Andrew is a police officer," Luke explained. Andrew obligingly dug into his pocket to produce his I.D. and badge.

Mrs. Simon threw up her arms, making a stalwart turnabout. "I wash my hands of the two of you!" she exclaimed.

Andrew grimaced. "Very biblical."

"Very," Luke agreed.

The phone rang, startlingly loud in the hospital quiet. Andrew picked up the receiver quickly. "Yes?"

He made a few noncommittal grunts and hung up, keeping his eyes on the phone rather than Luke.

"What?" Luke snapped.

Andrew at last looked at his brother. "She isn't at the house."

"Go on."

"Luke, your study has been torn to pieces. Nothing taken, just somebody looking for something."

"What else?" Luke asked flatly.

"A cabbie called into the station. Seems a lady had him drive her there, asked him to keep the meter running. She never came back out." He hesitated again, only a second. "The cabbie did see something he thought was a little strange, with hindsight. A van on the street, at night. And some guys dressed up like skiers hauling out some kind of carpet or something."

"Skiers! Hauling around carpeting? And he didn't know it was strange the minute he saw it?"

170

"You can see anything around here, and you know it, Luke," Andrew said softly. "The cabbie said something else."

"What?"

"He thought it was a trick of his eyes, but afterward . . . well, he said that the carpeting, or whatever it was, was moving."

The room seemed to spin again. The gray fog started to swamp around him, draining his strength. His knees felt like rubber.

"Luke!"

Andrew was at his side, holding him up. Luke shook his head; the gray slowly dispersed. He steadied and pulled himself free from his brother.

"Simson," he murmured.

"It can't be Simson. Simson has no connection with you! And I know for a fact that he's at the club where Tricia is singing. She checked in with me less than an hour ago."

"Andrew," Luke said tensely, "Simson has never had to be anywhere himself. He can hire half the hoods in the city. I'm telling you, Drew, this has something to do with Simson."

The phone started to ring again, shattering in the night, shrill. Andrew grabbed it before the first ring was completed. After his first yes, he remained silent, listening. Then he murmured, "We'll meet you out front."

He hung up the phone and stared at Luke. "Tricia just checked in from the club. Someone called Simson, and he left in a big hurry."

"Oh, God." Luke groaned.

"Let's go," Andrew said. "There will be an unmarked car waiting for us by the time we get downstairs."

Donna felt ill. The truck or van or whatever it was had lurched and turned in crazy zigzags for what had seemed like forever, always spewing gaseous fumes that now seemed to permeate even her flesh. The bedspread remained over her head, and it was difficult to breathe even the fumes.

At last the vehicle came to a halt. She felt herself being dragged and then lifted. She tried to kick and fight, but though the will was there, the strength was not. She tried to scream; all she issued were muted, garbled sounds.

She bounced about as she was carried down a length of stairs. It was cold now. Even with the spread about her, she felt a sharp, damp cold seeping through the fabric to her bones.

A moment later she was set down roughly on a frigid cement floor with her legs tangled beneath her. It was horrible. She couldn't see, and her arms were bound. Icy fingers of dampness wrapped around her with the terror of darkness that knew no alleviation. She tried to wrest the spread from about her head while working furiously at the bounds that secured her wrists.

"Just sit tight, preacher's woman!"

The soft laughter with its touch of cruelty could only belong to Red Cap. The spread, which she had managed to tear until she had almost dislodged it, was firmly replaced. She heard the sound of something cracking nearby and she jumped. Then she was touched again and she realized that he had only been removing his belt to better secure the spread over her eyes.

"You know, preacher's woman," he drawled softly, "so far, you just may get out of this okay. So far, you haven't seen anything. If I were you, I'd be mighty grateful that I hadn't."

Donna went rigid, saying nothing. A feeling of despair fell over her like a sheet of ice. She had no idea of where she was. She couldn't see and she couldn't move. The situation seemed beyond hopeless.

"You know what we want," the voice that was distinctively Red Cap's said.

She wanted to scream that she didn't know where Lorna was; she could do nothing but muffle out a protest.

"You've got her gagged!" Blue Cap muttered scornfully.

Donna recoiled as she felt Red Cap's fingers reach out for her again. The belt was loosened; she flinched as his hands crawled along her torso to her throat, and on to her mouth, wrenching the scarf away. Red Cap laughed again, apparently amused by her revulsion.

"Soft as satin and lush as fruit!" Red Cap taunted. "Seems like the preacher's got a good thing going."

Donna stiffened, determined not to dignify his words with a protest, determined not to flinch again.

"You can talk now," Red Cap said.

She could talk, but she couldn't see. Where was she? Somewhere, not far away, cars were driving about, horns were blaring. People were shouting. People. She opened her mouth and screamed as loud as she could.

A hand cuffed her against her cheek, the force of the blow muted by the covering over her head. It was still strong enough to make her see something other than darkness at last—an explosion of stars.

"Do it again," Red Cap hissed, "and I'll see that you're missing a few teeth—understand?"

Tears were flooding her eyes. She couldn't speak, nor would she nod. But she didn't make any more sounds.

"Where's the blonde?"

"I don't know," Donna answered dully.

"Lady, I don't think you realize how rough things could get."

"I'm telling you the truth. I don't know where she is."

Donna instinctively twisted as she heard a tapping coming from somewhere. She heard the shuffle of feet and then a whispered exchange. Then she heard a new voice. Refined, cultured. Deadly.

"Mrs. Trudeau. What a pity we've had to drag you here! I can't tell you how sorry I am for the inconvenience. If you would just be a little cooperative, we could send you on home."

Simson! The name seemed to scream in her mind. She didn't know how or why she knew it was that man, whom she had never met, she was just certain that it was he. . . .

Donna ground her teeth tightly together, trying not to shiver, desperately trying not to give way to the hysteria of panic.

"Mrs. Trudeau, I'm waiting. And I'm trying very hard to be patient. I'm just not a patient man."

"I don't know where she is. They wouldn't tell me. I swear to you, that's the truth."

Beneath the blanketing of the spread, Donna closed her eyes tightly. Thank God they had never told her. She was so frightened. She would have given it away.

But wherever Lorna was, *she* was protected. By the police. Donna was alone. And Luke . . . Luke was in the hospital. Drugged. Probably sleeping soundly. He wouldn't realize until morning that something was wrong.

"What do we do?" someone whispered uneasily. Donna was certain that it was Blue Cap. He didn't seem to mind being a

173

thief, but she was relieved that the thought of violence was disturbing to someone other than herself.

She heard a coarse laugh—Red Cap again. "If we're going to start with a little pressure, big guy, I can think of a lot of ways I'd like to apply it to the little lady."

She could bet he would! Donna thought heatedly. Anger faded with a rebirth of fear. What could she do if he touched her? Nothing!

"Oh, I don't think we need to take a chance on any . . . physical pressure yet, boys. I would think that if we left her alone for a while she might see reason."

"Leave her alone!" Red Cap protested.

"In the cellar," the man Donna assumed to be Simson said smoothly. "Do you have a cellar, Mrs. Trudeau? I'm sure you do. But I'll bet yours is fixed up nicely. A game room, maybe. Nice fireplace, maybe a bar. Or at the very least, you've probably got a nice laundry down there." She felt a hand brush against the area of her cheek. "Our cellar is quite different, Mrs. Trudeau. We've got rats. Big, fat ones. And I think I've seen spiders in every shade of the rainbow down there. Kind of pretty, actually. Rats . . . spiders . . . who knows what else? And it's cold, Mrs. Trudeau. Wet, and cold."

The man moved away. "Let her see our cellar, boys. If that doesn't convince her in a few hours that she wants to talk to me, she'll be all yours for a little friendly persuasion."

Hands gripped rudely at her again. She kicked and struggled against them. Then she went still as she felt a draft, and a scream, totally instinctive, ripped from her throat as she felt herself falling . . . bound . . . unable to break her fall.

"Scream down there all you like, Mrs. Trudeau. No one will hear you."

But she wasn't screaming anymore. The fall hadn't been all that damaging, but it had knocked the breath from her and she was stunned, gasping for air.

Vaguely she heard something snap shut. A trapdoor to the cellar?

She forgot about the door. She could hear other noises. Squeeks . . . the sounds of scurrying little footsteps. Rats. He hadn't lied, she was surrounded by rats.

Donna began to roll about insanely, desperately trying to free her face from the bedspread so that she could see.

Finally she managed to free herself from its blinding covering. Then she almost wished that she hadn't. It wasn't completely dark—not completely. A pale trace of light filtered through the closed door, enough so that she could see around her. Old cartons, old crates, a broken set of wooden stairs covered with cobwebs. Just as she was covered with cobwebs. They were in her hair, tangling over her face, covering her lips. She opened her mouth to scream, and the web seemed to fill her mouth. "God! *No!*"

Spitting and gagging, she fell against the concrete floor. It *was* cold. So cold. And damp. Seeping into her bones . . . into her spirit. Again she thought fleetingly of Lorna. Thank God that she didn't know where her friend was!

A feeling of sickness that made her gag and choke again came to her. This was only the beginning. Simson would turn her over to Red Cap when she didn't talk. . . .

The despair that set into her was almost overpowering. Tears of hysteria rose to her eyes again. She closed them tightly. Last night—last night at this time she had lain beside her husband's warmth, felt his passion, his strength, his tenderness . . . his love. She had been cherished. Tonight her bed was hard cement. Cold. Repelling. Her music was the squeal of rats, the only soft touch was that of a spider's web. . . .

Luke! He didn't even know! Wouldn't know. . . . Donna caught her breath suddenly. But maybe he would. Maybe he would. . . .

Her high rise of hope gave way to sinking despair. No. April had lost her life. And Luke hadn't been able to do a thing.

I can't give up! she raged inwardly as something scurried over her foot. She smothered a cry and slammed her boot against the floor.

She had to free her wrists. Grinding her teeth down hard together, Donna began to work at the bonds. She didn't stop to wonder what she would do if she managed to free herself; she didn't dare.

"Do you know how much time has passed?" Luke asked Andrew grimly as they drove down another street in the garment district.

"Luke, it's a big city. We're lucky we had a few witnesses to trace the van this far."

"Yeah," Luke murmured. This far, street after street, building after building stretched before them. Offices, factories, apartments. Thousands of little tiny cubicles where a woman could be hidden. His woman. His wife. . . .

It seemed as if Andrew was playing mind reader that night. "Luke, I know it appears vast, almost hopeless. But believe me, the streets are crawling with police. Marked cars, unmarked cars. Mounted patrol. A score of the best trained dogs available. We'll find her."

Luke wished that he could believe that Andrew had faith in his own words. He wished he could believe something but he couldn't. He felt nothing but desperation. Pain, fear, anxiety, and a horrible empty void where his "blind faith" should have been. He felt as he had all those years ago in the service, as if he had forgotten how to pray.

Where was everything? he wondered. The extra perception that had warned him of the danger had deserted him. His belief, the God he had thought he had come to know, was out of his reach. Fear had brought on bitterness, and he couldn't help but question all that had been his life, his faith, his belief. All that had been so very staunch. Even when he had lost April. He had known bitterness then, pain that cut like a knife. But he had lived through it. His faith had been there to sustain him then. But now even that was gone.

"Luke," Andrew urged in an anxiety-tinged tone. "Can't you . . . feel anything?"

Luke turned on his brother with a driving fury. "Damn it, Andrew! I wouldn't be sitting here like a log if I did! I've tried. And I've tried and I've—" He cut off his heated words. He hadn't prayed. He had forgotten how. "I'm sorry, Drew," he murmured flatly.

"Don't be," Andrew replied gruffly.

He pulled the old car he was driving around another corner. The sidewalks were empty. The street had an eerie feel to it. Empty. There were a lot of condemned buildings on the street.

176

Old places, tenements deserted by city edict. There were about eight million people in the city of New York; Andrew estimated there were about eight million rats and roaches living on this street alone. They were a long ways from Park Place.

"Andrew!" Luke gasped out suddenly, tersely.

"What?" Andrew snapped in return. He'd almost driven into a telephone pole, he'd jerked the wheel so abruptly.

Luke was still, his handsome features tense in the pale, false light.

"Luke!" Andrew said again. "What is it? Do you feel something? Sense something—what?"

Luke turned sharply to his brother. "Yes . . . I think."

"What? Where?"

"We're on the street. We're near. Straight ahead, Andrew, I'm certain."

Andrew allowed the engine to idle, then he began to creep along the street.

"There!" Luke suddenly exclaimed.

Andrew didn't see anything special, just another tenement.

"Where?"

Luke offered him a grim smile. "Nothing psychic, Andrew. Just a garage."

Andrew's heart thumped hard against his ribs. Beyond the tenement was some kind of an office building. With a garage. Where else would you hide a van?

He picked up the car's radio and called in their position. Luke was heading out of the car before he finished.

Andrew quickly rehooked the receiver. "Luke!"

Luke glanced back at him with annoyance. "I'm not a fool, Drew. I'll watch my step."

"I know. I just want you to wait. I'm coming with you."

She had never known that rats could be such bold creatures. They were *supposed* to run at the slightest sound. Not these rats. They stared at her in the darkness, their small, beady eyes like little rays of evil premonition. Donna returned those glares hatefully and thumped both boots hard against the floor again. The rats at last skittered and scratched away.

She tugged hard at the bonds about her wrists again, worrying at them with her fingers that were almost numb. So close to numb that once she had freed herself, it took her a moment to realize that she had done so.

Then her first action was to swipe her hands vigorously over her face to cleanse it the best she could of the cloying spider web. Thank God! She was free! Free in the cellar, at least. How long had she been down there? Long enough to feel as if the dampness had drenched her, to feel so cold that she didn't know if she could ever get warm again.

She stood quietly, staring at the slim rays of light coming from the trapdoor. Was there another entrance? There had to be. If not, they would be coming for her. And she could see now. If she saw them. . . . She didn't want to continue with the thought. Nor did she dare think of her fate if Red Cap got his hands on her. She couldn't think about rats or roaches. She had to crawl around and explore every inch of the cellar until she found something—a door, a window, a loose board. *Anything.*

She started moving. Spider webs brushed her hair again. She almost bumped into a support beam. She knelt down, discovering that she avoided a lot of the spider webs that way.

She kept crawling until she found a wall. It felt cold, but little colder than her own flesh. She moved on, running a hand along the wall. On and on. She recoiled in horror, stifling a scream as she touched something that moved. Swallowing deeply, she started to creep along again.

At last she touched something different. Not cement, but wood. Please God! She prayed silently. Let it be a street-level window, boarded up. *Loosely* boarded up.

She carefully located the boundaries of the wood. She had been right! There were several boards over a window. Ignoring the splinters that tore at her fingers, she began to tug at the boards. They were old, decaying, loose in her hands. She struggled for a firm grip on one and pulled for all that she was worth. It gave way, sending her flying back on her rear. And there was light beyond it. The murky gray light of night.

Donna stumbled back to her knees, peering through the long hole she had made. She couldn't possibly fit through it, but if she could tear off another board. . . . Her fingers explored and gripped the wood again. Then she paused, her heart racing with terror. There were voices again from above. A few sentences so low that she couldn't discern the words. And then another, crystal clear.

"Bring her up now."

Desperately she tugged at the board, ripping and tearing in mad panic.

The hatch door was thrown open. She heard it clunk and clatter as it was carelessly pushed aside. She turned her attention back to the board, pulling with all her strength as footsteps came down the rotting stairs. It was Red Cap. She knew it was he by his voice.

"Why, looky here! Our guest is trying to leave!"

He was a fairly young man, probably in his late twenties. But a long scar marred his cheek, and his eyes were as old and cruel as endless time.

Donna screamed, giving the board one last tug. This time it gave, but as she had before, she teetered backward with the momentum. Red Cap was coming closer and closer. She scrambled desperately to her feet, grabbing the board for protection. He kept coming toward her. She opened her mouth, screaming again, as loudly as she could. Long, and shrill. And desperate.

"Why, you little—"

He was coming straight toward her; suddenly he stopped. Donna realized he was looking beyond her.

A man was coming through the window. *Andrew!* It was Andrew! Oh, thank God!

Red Cap muttered an expletive, trying to spin about. Andrew was too quick for him. A flying leap brought him to Red Cap; the two crashed to the floor.

"Donna!"

Still too shocked to know the bliss of rescue, Donna barely recognized the voice. She turned, very slowly, as if she were in a dream.

"Luke!" His name tore in a wrenching anguish from her throat and she catapulted toward him. He engulfed her into arms that were strong and sure. Arms that were tender. Arms that convinced her she was really free at last.

"Are you all right?" He asked her hoarsely.

She nodded and was somewhat taken aback as he pushed her from him. But then she realized that Andrew was still scuffling with a man on the floor and that there was a commotion at the top of the stairs.

Luke ignored Andrew and went for the stairs.

And Donna was frightened again. For a brief second she had caught the glint of his eyes. She had never seen such fury or such ruthless purpose. But then he was gone. She heard oaths and grunts from above her, the sounds of a heavy weight falling and thumping against the floor.

"There are two of them!" She wanted to scream the belated warning but her voice was little more than a croak.

Apparently it didn't matter. The night was suddenly alive with the screeching wail of sirens, and when her knees buckled, someone was there to hold her. Another man. In a blue uniform. It seemed she was to be helped by men in blue uniforms all night.

Distantly, vaguely, she heard Andrew muttering out Red Cap's rights. Then she was prodded out the window and felt the cold again. But it was a beautiful cold. It came from the fresh air.

"Are you okay, Mrs. Trudeau?"

She barely saw the officer's face. She nodded at his words and discovered that she was sitting on a step, shivering. Then someone was shoving a cup of hot coffee in her hands.

There was so much commotion! And all she could do was sit and shiver until a blanket was wrapped around her shoulders. And something more. A touch she would know anywhere, at any time. Strong, sure, infinitely tender.

"You're cold."

She looked up into a pair of unique hazel eyes, green and gold, earth and fire. The fury was gone from them now; only tenderness remained.

"Luke?" she murmured anxiously. One of his eyes was circled with a puffy and darkening shadow.

"I'm fine," he said, sitting beside her and holding her close. He stared out into the night. "And Simson is . . . fine."

Donna shivered again. She wasn't sure what she felt. Yes, she did know what she felt. If Luke would have killed Simson, he would have been justified maybe in the eyes of the law. But not in his own heart.

He ruffled her hair gently. "He'll be charged with kidnapping for tonight, and because of tonight, they'll also be able to take him to court on the murder charges."

"I don't understand—"

"Tonight will make the charge much more plausible. It will substantiate all that Lorna can say on a witness stand."

"Oh," Donna mumbled.

"You're still shivering," he told her. "Are you that cold?"

She gazed into his eyes. "No, not when you're here."

He smiled, but his expression remained taut. "They're going to have to ask you a lot of questions tonight, Donna."

"I know," she said.

"The sooner we get started, the sooner we can get home."

"I'm ready," Donna replied.

Dawn was breaking in streaks of muted crimson and pale gray when they at last returned to the house. Donna was so tired that she was giddy. Luke seemed remarkably awake and alert. And lighthearted. In fact, as he closed the door behind them, he broke into laughter.

Donna stared at him, certain he had lost his mind.

His eyes continued to glitter as he returned her stare. Then he reached out a hand to touch her hair, arching a brow high. "Donna, I just realized what a disaster you are."

She saw her own reflection in the long hallway mirror. She *was* a disaster. Her hair was so full of dirt that it looked as if it had gone gray overnight. But she saw Luke's reflection too, and he definitely had a black eye.

"You don't look like such a deal yourself, you know," she retorted.

"I guess I don't," he said dryly. Then he gave her a grin that seemed doubly wicked because of the shiner. "I think we should take a shower."

"Luke! This has been the wildest, most terrifying, most horrendous night of my life! And you're—"

"Think of it this way, Donna," he murmured, wrapping his arms around her and pulling her length full against his. "Things can only go uphill from here."

She felt like laughing. But if she started laughing. . . .

"You're still supposed to be in the hospital," she reminded him.

181

"I've never felt better," he told her, and there was a ring of sincerity to his words that she didn't quite understand. But it was nice. Very nice.

He started walking, forcing her backward along the hall. "We really do need a shower."

"Really."

She wanted him. All of him. Next to her, holding her. Making love to her. Her eyes must have told him so because suddenly he wasn't leading her backward any more. He was lifting her into his arms and carrying her hurriedly down the hallway, to the door to their bedroom. She felt his heart beat, just as she felt her own. She saw the tension and the longing in his tautening features, in the gleam of fire in his eyes. A fire she had learned could warm her, no matter how cold she ever became.

He set her down in the bathroom and began to studiously tug at her sweater. Then at his own. Then they were helping one another, and their clothes were in a tumbled heap on the floor. Then there was the blessed cleansing relief of the water shooting down on them.

With the hard spray freeing her at last of the filth of the cellar, Donna turned about, encircling Luke's waist. The water continued to cascade over them.

"This should be wrong tonight," she murmured against his chest. "I mean, you should be in the hospital, exhausted—"

"I love you, Donna. And loving you can never be wrong." She felt a shudder ripple through his length. "Donna, I don't remember ever being so frightened in my life. Or feeling so alone. So panicked, so helpless. And then . . . we found you."

She pressed her lips against the delicious dampness of his chest. "I was never so terrified myself. How did you find me, Luke?"

She felt his shrug. He dipped, grabbing the soap. She felt it slide over her back, felt his fingers, massaging. . . .

"The taxi driver saw the van they took you in and a number of people noticed it on the street. It's a funny green color, and Simson's flunky was driving pretty badly. We found the district and then saw the garage. It was mostly logic."

"Oh," Donna murmured. "I had thought. . . ."

The soap paused against her spine. He caught her chin, tilting it to his. "I knew," he told her softly, "that something was wrong. But I don't think that was unique to me, not in this circumstance. When people love one another— Donna, tonight was many things. A police department that was right on the ball and knew its stuff. People who cared to get involved and volunteered information. And—" He smiled suddenly. "I like to think that there was a little divine intervention there. I felt like I had lost more than you. And . . ." He hesitated, then drew her sleek wet head tight against his slick chest. "When I found you, Donna, I found everything."

"Blind faith?"

"Blind faith."

A little sigh escaped her. She would never know exactly how he had found her, but all that really mattered was that he had.

"Donna?"

"Hmm?"

"You're not falling asleep on me, are you?"

"Uh-uh. I was just thinking. Luke, this means that Lorna can come out of hiding now too, doesn't it?"

He hesitated. "I think so, although I personally think she'll need to be very careful until Simson actually goes to trial. But I think I can safely promise that you can see her very soon."

"Tomorrow?"

"Probably," he murmured, moving his hands again. Soap suds were erotically smoothed over her hips and buttocks.

"That's wonderful."

"My touch? Or that you'll get to see Lorna?"

"Both!" Donna laughed.

"Mmm," Luke murmured dryly, refusing to give up his quest. A shivering sensation took hold of her despite the heat of the water. Despite that of his body. Or because of his body. He was pressed so close to her—so close that she could feel his rising desire, insinuating . . . exciting against her bare flesh.

The soap bar came between them. Along with the expert touch of his hands. She ached for that touch, and where she ached, it came. Her breasts were swathed with soap, caressed and cupped. Liquid quivers, as pulsating as the water, shot through her, centering low in her abdomen.

"There are benefits to having a half-psychic husband," he said.

"There are?" Donna queried. She lifted her eyes to his. They were heavy-lidded, sultry, sensual, the dark lashes thick and murky with tiny dewdrops of water.

"Hmmm. He knows . . . exactly where . . ."

"Oh, yes. . . ."

"To touch. . . ."

"To love. . . ."

Luke shuddered as her fingers began to move against him. He caught her lips in a deep kiss, tasting the water that cascaded around them and the sweetness that was her breath. Her nails lightly raked over his back, his buttocks. Her touch, wickedly sensual, found the evidence of his need.

"You're a little psychic yourself, love," he whispered against her lips.

"Not psychic—"

"Ahh, Donna. . . ."

"Just . . . in love. . . ."

"In the shower?"

"Mmmmmmmmm. . . ."

"Mmmmmmmmm. . . ."

The water continued to fall, a fast and furious crescendo as warm and luxuriously heated as the power and sweet passion of their love. It was the longest shower Donna had ever taken. And the most wonderful. When she had at last toweled herself dry, she slept more sweetly than she ever dreamed, more at peace, more serene and secure, in the arms of her husband and lover.

She awoke late, but she heard voices coming from the study. Yawning, she slipped into a robe and walked down the hall to the study.

Luke was talking to a man she didn't recognize at first; then she wondered how she possibly couldn't have recognized him. He was a handsome man. As tall as Luke, with hair as dark as Luke's rich jet. With eyes as green as an emerald sea. Clean shaven, dressed in an attractive suit.

"Andrew!" she exclaimed.

"Donna," he said apologetically. "I really am sorry. I shouldn't be disturbing you this morning. But—"

"Andrew," Donna murmured, hugging him and planting a kiss on his cheek before slipping into her husband's arms. She

184

smiled at him brightly. "After last night, Andrew Trudeau, you can crawl through my window any time you like."

He laughed. "I'm glad you said that. You never know. . . ." He lifted his hands with a grimace. "Actually, I'd glad you're awake. Tricia should be by to drop Lorna off at any minute."

"Wonderful!" Donna answered. As if on cue, the doorbell rang.

Luke gave her a little prod in the back. "I think that's for you."

She flashed him a smile and raced down the hall to the front door, throwing it open. A tall, lithe blonde stood there, smiling radiantly.

"Lorna!" Donna exclaimed. "Oh, Lorna, I've been so worried—"

"Donna! When I heard what had happened—"

They both broke off, hugging one another, laughing, hugging again. "Come on into the study!" Donna urged, pulling Lorna along. "Luke and—" She broke off as she entered the study. Luke was still there, smiling as he greeted Lorna affectionately, but there was no sign of Andrew. Donna raised a brow to Luke. He inclined his head briefly to the window. Apparently, her brother-in-law had left in customary fashion. Because of Lorna?

She didn't have long to wonder. There was so much to catch up on, so much to say, so much to hear.

Luke stayed awhile, then discreetly left them. Hours passed, but when Lorna rose to leave, Donna was dismayed.

"I've got a flight out to Boston tonight," Lorna explained. "They still wanted me to stay—they're worried about Simson pulling something before the trial. But I've got to get home, if only for a while."

"Be careful, Lorna," Donna pleaded.

Lorna promised to take the utmost care, but she was still anxious to get home.

Luke reappeared to say good-bye. He stood behind Donna, his arms wrapped around her, as Lorna was driven away.

Donna waved until she was waving at nothing. Then she turned around to face Luke, her smile a little sad.

"I'd thought . . . I don't know why exactly, but I'd thought there was something going on between Andrew and Lorna."

Luke smoothed her hair from her forehead, shrugging. "If it wasn't meant to be, Donna, it wasn't."

"He crawled back out of the window rather than see her, Luke."

"I know."

"Maybe they're both acting like fools."

"Maybe. Are you planning on some matchmaking? Because if you are, you know, it's a risky business. You should keep your little nose out of it."

"I'm going to try," Donna muttered, her eyes sparkling. "But, if I get a chance . . ."

Luke laughed. "Heaven protect us all! Donna, if there's something special between them, it's something they'll have to figure out for themselves."

"Do you think they will?" Donna asked worriedly.

Luke laughed. "I'm not a fortune teller, you know."

"Yes, I know," Donna said with a little grimace. Then she suddenly realized that she and Luke were finally free to get back to the business of day-to-day life. *Their* lives.

"I was just thinking, Luke, that this is Sunday. You should be at church!"

He smiled. "I have a very understanding employer."

"Oh?"

"Yes, I do." His grin broadened as he dipped to slip an arm beneath her knees and lift her high against him. "He understands completely that I love my wife, and I'm sure He heartily approves."

"Does He?"

"Definitely. Love is one of His favorite subjects."

She smiled, feeling totally luxurious as he carried her down the hall. "Luke?"

"Yes?"

"Did I ever tell you that you make me feel absolutely divine?"

"Heavenly?"

"Absolutely heavenly."

Fans of

Heather Graham

*will delight
in her boldest
romance to date!*

Golden Surrender

Against her will, Ireland's Princess Erin is married off by her father to her sworn enemy, Prince Olaf of Norway. A Viking warrior, Olaf and his forces are needed by the High King to defeat the invading Danes.

Nevertheless, the proud princess vows that her heart and soul will never belong to her husband, although her body might. Until one day that body, together with the life of her young baby, is almost destroyed by the evil Danes. When her husband *proves* his deep and abiding love for Erin by braving a desperate rescue attempt, she is forced to admit that her heart also holds a fierce love for her brave husband.
$3.50   12973-7-33

Don't forget Candlelight Ecstasies and Supremes for Heather Graham's other romances!

At your local bookstore or use this handy coupon for ordering:

DELL READERS SERVICE—DEPT. B745A
P.O. BOX 1000, PINE BROOK, N.J. 07058

Please send me the above title(s). I am enclosing $_____ (please add 75¢ per copy to cover postage and handling). Send check or money order—no cash or COD's. Please allow 3-4 weeks for shipment.
CANADIAN ORDERS: please submit in U.S. dollars.

Ms/Mrs/Mr _____

Address _____

City/State _____ Zip _____

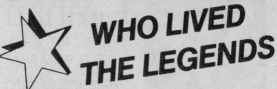

MEET THE STARS
⭐ WHO LIVED THE LEGENDS

_____ **BABY DOLL**, *Carroll Baker* 10431-9-17   3.95

_____ **BETTE**: The Life of Bette Davis
Charles Higham 10662-1-25   3.95

_____ **ELIZABETH TAYLOR**: The Last Star
Kitty Kelley 12410-7-42   3.95

_____ **INGRID BERGMAN**: My Story
Ingrid Bergman & Alan Burgess 14086-2-17   3.95

_____ **JOAN COLLINS, SUPERSTAR**: A Biography
Robert Levine 14399-3-19   3.50

_____ **KATHARINE HEPBURN**: A Hollywood Yankee
Gary Carey 14412-4-38   3.95

_____ **LANA**: The Public and Private Lives of Miss Turner
Joe Morella & Edward Z. Epstein 14817-0-13   3.50

_____ **RITA**: The Life of Rita Hayworth
Joe Morella & Edward Z. Epstein 17483-X-27   3.95

_____ **NATALIE**, *Lana Wood* 16268-8-12   3.95

At your local bookstore or use this handy coupon for ordering:

Dell **DELL READERS SERVICE—DEPT. B745B**
P.O. BOX 1000, PINE BROOK, N.J. 07058

Please send me the above title(s). I am enclosing $_____ (please add 75¢ per copy to cover
postage and handling). Send check or money order—no cash or COOs. Please allow 3-4 weeks for shipment.
<u>CANADIAN ORDERS</u>: please submit in U.S. dollars.

Ms./Mrs./Mr _____

Address _____

City/State _____ Zip _____

Ever fantasize about having a mad, impetuous

FLING

Sensuous. Discreet. Astonishingly passionate, but with <u>no strings</u> attached? Kelly Nelson did, as she approached her 32nd birthday, so her two best friends arranged a one-night fling as a surprise present. Only problem was that Kelly, accustomed to juggling the demands of a solid marriage, two children, and a successful career, wasn't prepared for what happened next. Neither were her two best friends...her kids...her husband...or her incredibly sensitive, sensuous lover.

by PAMELA BECK and PATTI MASSMAN

12615-0-11   **$3.95**

As advertised on TV

At your local bookstore or use this handy coupon for ordering:

DELL READERS SERVICE—DEPT. B745C
P.O. BOX 1000. PINE BROOK. N.J. 07058

Please send me the above title(s). I am enclosing $_____ (please add 75¢ per copy to cover postage and handling). Send check or money order—no cash or COODs. Please allow 3-4 weeks for shipment.
<u>CANADIAN ORDERS: please submit in U.S. dollars.</u>

Ms./Mrs./Mr._____

Address_____

City/State_____ Zip_____

ON LEAVING CHARLESTON

ALEXANDRA RIPLEY

Live this
magnificent
family saga
—from the
civilized,
ante-bellum South
through the wreckless,
razzle-dazzle Jazz Age

Southern heiress Garden Tradd sheds the traditions
of her native Charleston to marry the rich, restless
Yankee, Sky Harris. Deeply in love, the happy young
couple crisscross the globe to hobnob with society in
Paris, London, and New York. They live a fast-paced,
fairy-tale existence, until the lovely Garden discovers
that her innocence and wealth are no insulation against
the magnitude of unexpected betrayal. In desperation
the gentle woman seeks refuge in the city she had once
abandoned, her own, her native land—Charleston.

$3.95   16610-1-17

Catch
SPRING
FEVER
with Dell

As advertised on TV

Dell

At your local bookstore or use this handy coupon for ordering:

DELL READERS SERVICE—DEPT. B745D
P.O. BOX 1000, PINE BROOK, N.J. 07058

Please send me the above title(s). I am enclosing $_____ (please add 75¢ per copy to cover
postage and handling). Send check or money order—no cash or COOs. Please allow 3-4 weeks for shipment.
CANADIAN ORDERS: please submit in U.S. dollars.

Ms./Mrs./Mr._____

Address_____

City/State_____ Zip _____

Candlelight
Ecstasy Romances™

- ☐ **274 WITH ALL MY HEART,** Emma Merritt 19543-8-13
- ☐ **275 JUST CALL MY NAME,** Dorothy Ann Bernard 14410-8-14
- ☐ **276 THE PERFECT AFFAIR,** Lynn Patrick 16904-6-20
- ☐ **277 ONE IN A MILLION,** Joan Grove 16664-0-12
- ☐ **278 HAPPILY EVER AFTER,** Barbara Andrews 13439-0-47
- ☐ **279 SINNER AND SAINT,** Prudence Martin 18140-2-20
- ☐ **280 RIVER RAPTURE,** Patricia Markham 17453-8-15
- ☐ **281 MATCH MADE IN HEAVEN,** Malissa Carroll 15573-8-22
- ☐ **282 TO REMEMBER LOVE,** Jo Calloway 18711-7-29
- ☐ **283 EVER A SONG,** Karen Whittenburg 12389-5-15
- ☐ **284 CASANOVA'S MASTER,** Anne Silverlock 11066-1-58
- ☐ **285 PASSIONATE ULTIMATUM,** Emma Merritt 16921-6-11
- ☐ **286 A PRIZE CATCH,** Anna Hudson 17117-2-13
- ☐ **287 LOVE NOT THE ENEMY,** Sara Jennings 15070-1-46
- ☐ **288 SUMMER FLING,** Natalie Stone 18350-2-41
- ☐ **289 AMBER PERSUASION,** Linda Vail 10192-1-16

$1.95 each

At your local bookstore or use this handy coupon for ordering:

DELL READERS SERVICE—DEPT. B745E
P.O. BOX 1000, PINE BROOK, N.J. 07058

Please send me the above title(s). I am enclosing $_____ (please add 75¢ per copy to cover postage and handling.) Send check or money order—no cash or CODs. Send check or money order—no cash or CODs. Please allow 3-4 weeks for shipment.

Ms./Mrs./Mr _____

Address_____

City/State_____ Zip_____

All-new
Candlelight Newsletter

An exceptional, *free* offer awaits readers of Dell's incomparable Candlelight Ecstasy and Supreme Romances.

Subscribe to our all-new CANDLELIGHT NEWSLETTER and you will receive—at absolutely no cost to you—exciting, exclusive information about today's finest romance novels and novelists. You'll be part of a select group to receive sneak previews of upcoming Candlelight Romances, well in advance of publication.

You'll also go behind the scenes to "meet" our Ecstasy and Supreme authors, learning firsthand where they get their ideas and how they made it to the top. News of author appearances and events will be detailed, as well. And contributions from the Candlelight editor will give you the inside scoop on how she makes her decisions about what to publish—and how *you* can try your hand at writing an Ecstasy or Supreme.

You'll find all this and more in Dell's CANDLELIGHT NEWSLETTER. And best of all, *it costs you nothing*. That's right! It's Dell's way of thanking our loyal Candlelight readers and of adding another dimension to your reading enjoyment.

Just fill out the coupon below, return it to us, and look forward to receiving the first of many CANDLELIGHT NEWSLETTERS—overflowing with the kind of excitement that only enhances our romances!

Dell DELL READERS SERVICE—DEPT. B745F
P.O. BOX 1000, PINE BROOK, N.J. 07058

Name_____

Address_____

City_____

State_____ Zip_____